Also by Randy Wayne White

SHARKS INCORPORATED

Fins

STINGERS

SHARKS INC.

RANDY WAYNE WHITE

ROARING BROOK PRESS
New York

Published by Roaring Brook Press
Roaring Brook Press is a division of Holtzbrinck Publishing Holdings Limited
Partnership
120 Broadway, New York, NY 10271 • mackids.com

Library of Congress Cataloging-in-Publication Data
Names: White, Randy Wayne, author.
Title: Stingers / by Randy Wayne White.
Description: New York : Roaring Brook Press, 2021. | Series: Sharks
    incorporated ; book 2 | Audience: Ages 8 to 12. | Audience: Grades 4–6.
Summary: While in the Bahamas with Doc Ford, who is investigating
    invasive lionfish, Maribel, Luke, and Sabina find precious artifacts but
    outlaws learn of their find and come after them.
Identifiers: LCCN 2020042081 (print) | LCCN 2020042082 (ebook) |
    ISBN 9781250244635 (hardcover) | ISBN 9781250244642 (ebook)
Subjects: CYAC: Adventure and adventurers—Fiction. | Buried
    treasure—Fiction. | Bahamas—Fiction.
Classification: LCC PZ7.1.W4466 Sti 2021 (print) | LCC PZ7.1.W4466
    (ebook) | DDC [Fic]—dc23
LC record available at https://lccn.loc.gov/2020042081
LC ebook record available at https://lccn.loc.gov/2020042082

Our books may be purchased in bulk for promotional, educational, or business use. Please contact your local bookseller or the Macmillan Corporate
and Premium Sales Department at (800) 221-7945 ext. 5442 or by email at
MacmillanSpecialMarkets@macmillan.com.

First edition, 2021 • Book design by Cassie Gonzales
Printed in the United States of America by LSC Communications, Harrison-
burg, Virginia

10   9   8   7   6   5   4   3   2   1

For the Barracuda Swim Club of Cat Island
and four gifted eco guardians:
Ryder & Layla Grissom and Ella Mae & Jessa Rosenbaum

A Note from the Author

The islands of Sanibel, Captiva, and the Bahamas are real places, faithfully described but used fictitiously in this novel. The same is true of certain businesses, marinas, hotels, and other places frequented by Dr. Ford, Hannah, and the members of Sharks Incorporated.

In all other respects, however, this novel is a work of fiction. Names (unless used by permission), characters, places, and incidents are either the product of the author's imagination or are used fictitiously. Any resemblance to actual persons, living or dead, or to actual events or locales is unintentional and coincidental.

For more information, visit docford.com.

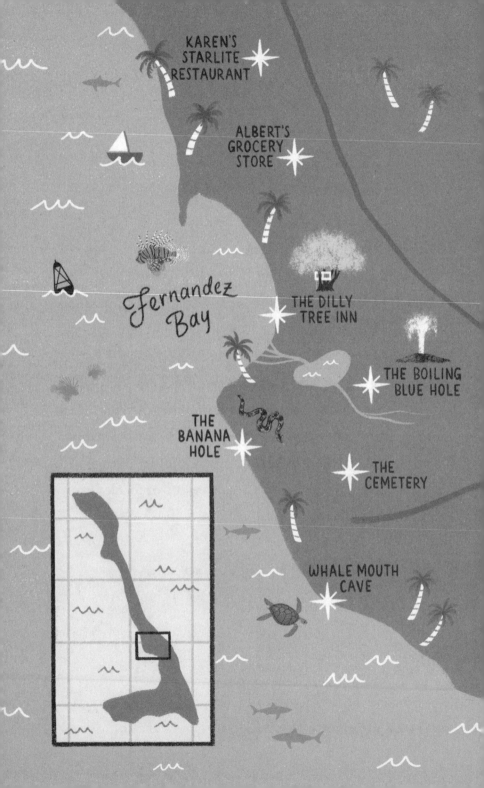

Ghosts aren't like the ones in cartoons. They have bodies, they eat food, they love. But they're haunted souls, because they're just visiting. Trying to finish unfinished business. Most of them died too young. I meet ghosts all the time. Everyone does.

—inspired by S. M. Tomlinson,
in the Doc Ford novel *Dark Light*

ONE

SHARKS INCORPORATED
IN THE BAHAMAS

They flew from Florida in a small plane, east over the Bahama Islands, into a watercolor nation of blue.

"Lots of small sharks down there," biologist Dr. Marion Ford said. "The big ocean sharks usually stay in deep water. Remember that. I don't want you kids messing around in deep water. We only have one rule—and you know what that rule is."

He sat at the controls. To his right was Maribel Estéban, age thirteen. She was tall, studious, quiet, and always, always dependable.

"It's an easy rule to remember," Maribel said. She opened the spiral notebook she'd purchased just for this trip and made a notation.

Strapped into the back seats were her ten-year-old sister, Sabina, and their friend Lucas Jones, age eleven.

It was noisy inside the plane. They all wore radio headphones.

"There it is—Katt Island," the biologist said. "Let's take a closer look."

Hills of green appeared in the front windshield. The hills were joined by strands of silver beach.

Like a slow roller coaster, the little plane tilted downward. The doors were made of some type of plastic glass. A hundred feet below, the water was clear. Shadows of fish glided over white sand.

"What kind of sharks?" Maribel asked.

"Can't tell from here," the biologist replied. "Couple of turtles, too. The whole island is a nursery for all kinds of sea life. And plenty of sharks to tag. You kids are gonna love it here."

"I already do," Sabina said into her microphone.

Usually, the ten-year-old girl had her nose buried in a book, or was writing poems in her diary. Not now. The scenery was too beautiful. And they were here to work. Over the summer, she, her sister, and Luke had learned how to tag and release small sharks. It was a research program designed for schoolkids.

Doc, the biologist, had been a fun but demanding teacher. The same was true of his partner, Captain Hannah Smith. Hannah was Luke's aunt. She was a famous fishing guide.

The kids had become a team—Sharks Incorporated. They had learned to work quickly and professionally. As a team, they had tagged and released more than one hundred small sharks near their homes on Sanibel Island, Florida. Luke, Maribel, and Sabina had also earned a fifty-thousand-dollar reward for helping to bust a gang of shark poachers.

The money had gone into the bank, of course. This trip to the Bahamas was a bonus. They had been invited to spend three weeks on this remote island off the Florida coast. The kids would tag sharks, and learn about sea turtles and other wildlife in the island nation of the Bahamas.

The Commonwealth of the Bahamas was the official name.

Doc was here for a different reason. Coral reefs in the area were being destroyed by invaders. *Lionfish*, the invaders were called. Unlike sharks, lionfish seldom weighed more than a few pounds. But they were terribly destructive—and dangerous, too.

The three young members of Sharks Incorporated would help Doc with his research.

The little blue-and-white seaplane banked to the left. It gained speed, then swooped upward. Katt Island, lined by cliffs and white sand, grew larger.

"That's where you'll be staying," the biologist said. "Hannah's there now, and I'll be back as soon as I can."

Below was a cluster of cabins shaded by coconut palms. There were no other houses for miles. A narrow road cut through hills and ragged trees. South, where the beach ended, was a rocky cliff that dropped into the sea.

The plane climbed higher and circled. Seeing the area from the air was a lot better than looking at a satellite photo on a computer screen. Katt Island was long and narrow, with what resembled a boot at the bottom.

"Looks like a pirate's boot," Sabina said. "Is that a cemetery down there in those trees?"

When the biologist laughed, their radio earphones crackled with static.

"Could be. You're right about pirates," he said. "That island is loaded with caves. There are a lot of legends about treasure being hidden down there. The real treasure, though, is the people who live on Katt Island. And the clear water."

A moment later, he said, "Hang on. Let's fly low over the lagoon."

"I love pirates and cemeteries." Sabina grinned. "What's a lagoon?"

"You'll see," the man replied.

Luke's stomach fluttered when the plane dived toward the water. Below was a salty lake. The lake was connected to the ocean by jade-colored creeks no wider than sidewalks. The creeks tunneled through acres of low trees.

A speck of swirling black water grabbed the boy's attention. The speck resembled a hole in the earth. It lay in a basin of sand, not far from the cabins where they would be staying.

A cave? he wondered.

Sabina was still thinking about pirates. Within a few days, her curiosity would lead the kids to the oldest cemetery on Katt Island. There they would discover a hundred-year-old mystery.

Luke remained focused on the dark spot that looked like a hole in the earth. He had no way of knowing that his curiosity about that strange hole would nearly get him killed.

Maribel, sitting in the copilot seat, looked down at the lagoon and the rocky green hills. In her spiral notebook, she wrote, *Sharks Incorporated has just one simple rule: Always follow all rules, but above all else take care of your teammates.*

On the next line, she wrote the date and added, *Flying into the Bahamas is like flying into a beautiful blue dream.*

TWO
LOST!

After a few days on Katt Island, the last thing Luke expected when he left his cabin that morning was to end up trapped in the swirling black hole he'd seen from the airplane.

But that's what happened.

Problem was, he'd grown up on a farm. He was always awake before Maribel and Sabina, who slept in the little cabin next to his. So, at sunrise, he grabbed a granola bar and went down the steps while roosters crowed, and parrots quarreled in the trees.

Breakfast was an hour away. Plenty of time to explore.

All week, he'd been thinking about the speck of swirling black water he'd seen from Doc's seaplane. But he hadn't had time to search for the spot. He and the sisters had been too busy learning about lionfish and sea turtles and coral reefs. Most mornings, there was work to do. And afternoons were spent tagging small sharks in the shallows.

This was Luke's first free morning—a chance to explore on his own.

Smoke from a cooking fire trailed him across the empty beach toward the bay. A lagoon, the biologist had called it. Never had the boy seen water so clear and blue.

Carrying a mask, a snorkel, and his expensive new Rocket fins, Luke waded out. He sealed the mask over his face and dived under.

The world of sunlight became an aquarium of tiny fish, rainbow colors.

A sea turtle appeared. It was the size of a dinner plate, its shell golden-green. Long flippers stroked the water like wings as it glided past.

Wow. In the Bahamas, turtles were fast! They were nothing like the plodding turtles found in farm ponds. Sea turtles soared in clear water like birds, even when the water was only a few feet deep.

Luke, wearing rubber booties inside his new fins, followed at a distance. That was just how he was. The boy's eyes would lock on to an object while his mind forgot everything else. Next thing he knew, he'd be lost, miles from where he started, with not a clue how long he'd been gone, or how to get back.

It had happened to him many times, growing up on a small farm west of Toledo, Ohio. And never did he bother to tell anyone where he was going.

Fact was, Luke seldom knew himself.

Brain-dead, his stepfather had termed the flaw before sending Luke to Florida to live with his aunt, Captain Hannah Smith.

That was four months ago.

The same was true on this bright blue morning in the Bahamas. The turtle didn't seem to mind being followed. Occasionally, it would pause to munch on blades of underwater grass. This gave the boy time to stand up, clean his mask, and look around.

When he first stopped, his little tree-house cabin was still visible. A few stops later, he was alone in the shallow blue lagoon. The sandy bottom was tinted bronze. The area was pocked with mangroves, rubbery trees that thrived in saltwater. The mangroves blocked his view of the cabins. But as the turtle sailed through an opening in the trees, the boy followed.

Water deepened, but not much. The next time the turtle stopped, Luke could stand up, no problem. A *tidal creek*— that was how locals referred to the streams that ribboned through the lagoon.

Tide was a word most farm kids didn't understand. Luke did, sort of, because his aunt was a fishing guide. And the biologist, Dr. Ford, was his closest adult friend.

Here was how tides worked: Twice a day, almost every day, seawater flooded into the bays until the tide was high. Twice a day, almost every day, it flowed back into the sea. At low tide, the water might reach only to your ankles. At high tide, the water might be up to your chest. Both tides, high and low, peaked a little later every day of the week.

Usually by about an hour, the boy had been told.

It had something to do with the moon.

The tide was flooding in from the sea when Luke left that morning. The current was mild. The flow carried him and the turtle along at an easy pace. It didn't seem like an hour, but probably was.

There was a lot to see—including lionfish. They were strange-looking creatures with ornate stingers. The stingers fanned out from their bodies like a lion's mane. The name *lionfish* made sense.

Lionfish didn't belong in the Bahamas, he and the sisters had learned. They were native to the Pacific Ocean, but had somehow traveled halfway around the earth.

More likely, they had escaped from a resort's giant aquarium, Doc had told them.

Lionfish had no natural enemies in this part of the world. They were multiplying like crazy. Worse, they were killing all types of local sea life. Lionfish weren't aggressive, but touch one? *Ouch.* Their sting was incredibly painful. Sometimes even deadly.

Luke was careful not to get too close when he swam past them.

As he followed the turtle, a couple of barracudas shadowed him for a while. A few days ago, the boy would've been spooked by their daggerlike teeth.

Not now. He had gotten used to swimming with 'cudas. The lagoon, they had learned, was a nursery for small sea creatures of all types. Bigger, sometimes dangerous fish—including sharks—hunted outside the reef in deep water.

Sure, you still had to keep an eye out for jellyfish and stingrays. They didn't attack, but, like lionfish, they had dangerous stingers.

The boy was reminded of this when, ahead, a stingray

exploded from the sand. It surprised the turtle, too. This caused the creature to zoom from sight at an incredible speed.

The turtle resembled a golden Frisbee with fins. That image stuck in Luke's head. He stood, spit in his mask, and for the first time wondered how far he had traveled from the cabin.

No idea.

He noticed, though, that the current was now flowing in a different direction. It was stronger. Much stronger.

Maybe this was good. It meant the tide had changed. Water was streaming out of the shallows, returning to the sea. The same current that had carried him into the lagoon might carry him back to the cabins where they were staying.

Makes sense, Luke thought.

He had already missed breakfast, so he needed to hurry. Every day at lunch, he and the Estéban sisters were expected to meet and go over their schedule. They still had a lot to learn about Katt Island.

Today, something special had been planned. His aunt, Captain Hannah, was supposed to take them to a place where they might be able to see giant sharks from the shore.

Soon the lagoon was too shallow to swim. Luke, after taking off his swim fins, started walking.

No idea which way to go. He was lost. What had been a blue aquarium was now a desert of sand. Worse, if he didn't hurry, he'd miss the noon meeting.

Maribel, the quiet sister, was nice enough to be understanding if he was late.

Not Sabina. The ten-year-old had a sharp tongue—and a temper. And she often kidded Luke about growing up on a farm. Which was okay. Usually.

He liked both girls. Trusted them, too. It was probably like having sisters of his own, because Sabina, especially, could be a pain in the rump. But he dreaded the embarrassment if they found out that he was lost again.

Ahead, the boy noticed something strange. There was a deep blue shadow where water appeared to not just bubble. It boiled, like water in a cauldron. But there was no steam, so the water wasn't hot.

Was it the swirling black hole he had spotted from the airplane?

This was exciting. Wearing his rubber dive boots, he slogged closer. It wasn't a shadow. It was a bubbling whirlpool. Luke pictured a flushing toilet—the way the tide swirled was similar. The whooshing suction sound it made was familiar, too.

Luke would have detoured around the spot if he hadn't seen a turtle rocket past his knees. It was followed by another . . . then another.

You're not going to lose me this time, he thought.

An instant later, the boy was spinning in circles. The current pulled him down, down, down into a hole beneath the water.

THREE
VULTURES IN A DREAM

Sabina, who was only ten, knew Maribel wouldn't believe her, but she tried to convince her older sister anyway. "Luke is lost again," she said in Spanish. "I followed his footprints to the beach. His snorkel gear is gone, and he missed breakfast. That's not like him."

Spanish was their native language. More than a year ago, the Estéban sisters had left Cuba on a homemade raft. Cuba was a large, beautiful island nation south of Florida. They probably would have died if Dr. Ford hadn't come by in his boat.

Since surviving that trip, the sisters looked at life differently than most people—adults and kids alike. They were happy just to be alive.

"You know how Luke is," Sabina continued. "He walks around with an empty head until his stomach's just as empty. That farm boy has a nose like a dog. He would've smelled the pancakes."

Maribel didn't want to overreact. "It's only a little after ten," she said. "We don't meet until noon."

"What about later, though?" the younger sister said. "Captain Hannah is taking us to see big sharks from shore. If Luke's lost, he might spoil everything."

Maribel remained calm. "This is Luke's first morning off since we got here. It's none of our business what he does when he's alone. How would you like it if he followed your tracks around the island?"

"As if he cares enough to bother," Sabina shot back. "If he followed anyone, it would be you—you're everybody's favorite. The prettiest, the tallest. You never get in trouble. No one pays attention to me."

Maribel said patiently, "That's mean. And it's not true." She switched to English, to practice both languages. "Besides, we have work to do."

The girl carried her spiral notebook and a small waterproof camera. Most mornings, it was their job to walk the beach and makes notes about what they saw. The trio took turns every day, exploring the island when they weren't on turtle duty.

It was important to document sea-turtle nests on the beach. The nests were easily spotted. Tractor-like tracks led to messy circles dug in the sand. The biologist had already warned them that thieves sometimes robbed the nests of eggs or baby turtles. Someone had to record any changes before the turtles hatched.

They also had to make notes if they saw one or more lionfish. Lionfish resembled small rocks covered with beautiful flowing hair. And they usually hunted in packs.

After almost a week on Katt Island, the girls knew that lionfish were seldom found along the beach. The fish preferred to hide near corals, colorful rocks that were actually living creatures.

"No lionfish here," Maribel said. She made a note in her notebook. "We have two more spots to check. Come on."

Sabina glowered. She fingered the necklace she always wore. The beads were tiny seashells called cowries. "Whatever," she grumbled, trying out her American slang. Then she spoke more slowly, because she sometimes had trouble choosing the right words in English. "Luke is either lost or he's done something dumb—typical for a pig farmer from

Ohio. You'll see. Don't blame me if vultures eat him before lunch."

"Vultures?" Maribel tried not to smile.

"Yes, with nasty black eyes. Last night, those ugly birds came to me in a dream."

Sabina often had strange dreams. Occasionally, the girl got so involved with the dreams that she walked in her sleep. That could be dangerous.

Maribel was amused until her sister added, "Or what if he gets struck by lightning again? You know how storms follow that boy around."

When it came to Luke, thunderstorms were a worry. Three months ago, in Florida, he'd been zapped by a lightning bolt. He might have died. Instead he'd spent weeks being tested by experts, and he still had feathery burn scars on his hand and shoulder.

The boy, according to his aunt Hannah, had acted different ever since. He would drift off in dreamy silences. Sometimes he claimed to hear and see what others could not.

That part, both sisters believed.

Doctors who had tested Luke's brain said that lightning had nothing to do with the boy's unusual eyesight. His eyes and his excellent hearing were natural gifts, they insisted. But it was true that Luke's dreamy wanderings often led him into trouble.

Maribel started to say, "If he's not here by noon, I'll tell Captain Hannah, and—"

A local girl, Tamarin Rowland, came toward the sisters. She waved her arms and yelled, "Birds, they eating all the baby turtles! Y'all gotta come and help me. They be soon gone if we don't."

It was August. Sea-turtle eggs buried on the beach were finally hatching. The girls had photographed several nests, but they had never seen baby turtles before.

"What can we do?" they asked in unison.

Tamarin was tall and wore jeans. A red bandanna was knotted around her beautifully braided hair. She motioned and sprinted away, calling out in her Bahamian accent, "Co' mon! 'Urry, 'urry."

Sabina got a head start. Maribel, with her long legs, could've caught up but didn't. She trailed her sister and Tamarin around a rocky point to the ocean side of the island.

Suddenly, all three girls stopped. On the beach was a

horrible sight. Big birds with leathery heads had gathered in a mob. They were feasting on the newly hatched turtles that streamed toward the sea.

There were hundreds of baby turtles, their shells the size of walnuts. They resembled a herd of confused crabs as the birds stabbed at them with their beaks.

"Poor little things," Tamarin cried. "They should'a waited and hatched on the Turtle Moon like most do."

The Turtle Moon? The sisters didn't know what this meant. There wasn't time to ask.

Tamarin spun around and ordered, "Y'all grab conch shells to throw. Those birds are vultures. They eat anything. We've got to scare them away."

Conch, pronounced "konk," were sea creatures with large, heavy shells. Conch was a favorite food in the Bahamas. The old shells were piled everywhere.

To demonstrate, the local girl hurled a conch shell, grabbed another, and charged.

The vultures didn't care. They waddled, wings outstretched. They lifted themselves into the air only to land a few yards away. Immediately, the birds resumed stabbing the sand and swallowing the tiny turtles.

Tamarin threw another conch shell and a chunk of

wood. Sabina and Maribel joined in, throwing whatever they could find. The results were the same. The birds hissed. They flapped out of range, then waddled back and continued eating turtles.

"They're not afraid." Sabina frowned. "We've got to think of something else."

Tamarin snapped her fingers and ran to the coconut trees along the beach. She returned dragging three palm fronds that had fallen from the trees. Each frond was six feet long and feathered with leaves.

"Try waving them like fans," she said. "They'll make us seem bigger. You know, like more of a threat."

It worked. The girls marched along with the hatchlings. They fanned the turtles as the tiny things scrambled toward the water. If a vulture was too bold, the branches became prods that scared the bird away.

Back and forth the girls went, escorting baby turtles from the beach to the sea.

Maribel marveled at the courage of these newborns. Only minutes after hatching, the turtles knew exactly what they had to do—get to the water. Their tiny fins were as delicate as feathers, yet they plowed steady furrows over shells and sand.

"Shoo . . . get out of here!" Sabina yelled when a pair of vultures soared too close.

The birds veered away and spattered her shoulder with something wet. Chunks of baby turtle, Sabina thought, but she knew better when she sniffed her shirt.

"Oh . . . gag. Those birds pooped on me!" she yelled.

Maribel had to cover her mouth to keep from laughing. Tamarin tried to hold it in, too, but gave up.

"It's not funny," Sabina sputtered.

She charged the nearest vulture and missed with the branch she swung. These tall, solemn birds scared her, the way they hissed and clacked their beaks. They reminded the girl of black-hooded gnomes she had seen in picture books.

When most of the baby turtles had made it to the water, Sabina thought of something else. "Remember what I dreamed about last night?" she said to Maribel. "*Vultures*. In my dream, I thought they had something to do with Luke. I'm sure he's lost."

The sisters stared at each other for a moment. It was Maribel who said, "You're right. Tamarin grew up on this island. Maybe she can help us find him before we all get in trouble."

FOUR
ESCAPE FROM THE BOILING BLUE HOLE

Luke's eyes had adjusted to the darkness of the hole he'd fallen into. It was a hollow chamber, like a cave. Instead of flooding the chamber, water showering past his head continued downward into what seemed to be a bottomless hole. Rock walls were jagged. The ledge that had stopped his fall was narrow.

After a few minutes, the waterfall spilling from above began to slow. The boy's breathing returned to normal. His dive mask was still around his neck, but one of his expensive swim fins was missing.

Where had it gone?

Luke looked down into the bluest darkness he'd ever

seen. If he slipped, how far would he fall? Ten feet? A thousand?

I've got to find a way out of here! he thought.

He began to search for flat slabs of rock. If he piled the rocks high enough, he might be able to stand and reach the opening.

As he worked, the drizzling waterfall stopped completely.

Low tide, he thought.

Luke was right. Even though he understood how tides worked, he didn't realize the danger he was in.

Soon, water began flooding upward from below the boy's feet. Slowly, at first, then faster and faster. The tide had changed. Water was now flowing in from the sea. It was like someone deep inside the earth had turned on a fire hose.

The boy continued to add slabs of limestone to the pile, but the water was soon up to his knees.

I'm trapped, he thought. *If I don't get out, I'll drown.*

Luke panicked. In a rush, he braced his hands against the wall. He stepped up onto the pile of rocks he had built. The rocks were slippery and sharp. They sliced into the soles of his flimsy boots. When the boy lunged for the sunny opening, he lost his balance and tumbled backward.

Splash!

Instead of falling, he landed in a churning whirlpool. The water circled and lifted him. He sculled with his hands to stay on the surface. Around and around he went, banging into rocks as the water floated him upward.

This was a good thing, the boy realized. He didn't have to climb out of the chamber. He could swim out if the tide continued to flood the hole from below.

That's what happened. Sort of.

Above Luke's head, the sunny opening spun around. He reached . . . got both hands on the limestone, and pulled himself up. Then he hung there despite rocks cutting into his chest. Suddenly, the flood of blue water gushed like a fountain. Luke went sailing out of the hole. He landed on his knees in the sandy lagoon.

It was like waking up from a bad dream. The dive mask was still around his neck, but now both swim fins were missing. Had they been sucked down into the earth?

He walked toward the crevice. Because of the way the water bubbled, he thought of it as the Boiling Blue Hole.

At least one of his fins was still down there. But what about the other fin?

Luke stopped abruptly. He saw a caution light sparking in his head and decided, *No way, man.* He wasn't going to get trapped again.

Since being struck by lightning, Luke had changed. Behind his eyes was a private space. It contained a bright circle of blue. He could sometimes focus the circle like a telescope. Words had colors—numbers, too. He could see and hear what few other people could.

The nice doctors who had tested his brain didn't credit lightning for these changes.

Luke did. And he had come to trust his "lightning eye," especially when it came to danger.

The boy stepped back, and there it was—his missing swim fin. It lay in the sand nearby. But the other fin had definitely been sucked down into the Boiling Blue Hole.

Luke tucked the fin under his arm. He did a slow turn. Which way was the cabin? The sun was high in the sky. It had to be close to noon.

Well . . . darn it. Katt Island was small—only two miles wide by the lagoon. There had to be a road or a beach around here somewhere. So he started off, with no idea where he was, then suddenly halted.

Behind him, from far away, came the sound of girls' voices. He heard the word *vultures* and an occasional yelp. This suggested the girls were angry about something.

Maribel and Sabina were probably looking for him.

Crapola, he thought. He sloshed toward the voices, determined to find the girls before *they* found him. How else could he prove he'd never been lost at all?

Ahead was a hill and a limestone ridge. The hill was covered with witchy-looking trees. He stopped again. Instead of the girls, he heard the muted howling of a dog. The howling was coming from the same direction as the girls' voices—somewhere atop the ridge.

Luke sensed an animal in trouble. Luke got along with animals a lot better than he did people.

At a run, he high-stepped through the shallows.

FIVE

DRAGONS AND MONEY TROUBLE

People in the Bahamas had a musical way of speaking. Their accent was beautiful, yet sometimes difficult to understand. That's why the Estéban sisters were confused when Tamarin said, "Luke might've enjoyed himself some small kind'a trouble, skylarking back there in the lagoon."

"What kind of trouble?" Sabina asked. "We were told there's nothing that lives in the lagoon to be afraid of."

Tamarin replied in a spooky tone, "That's right. Nothing that *lives* there."

Maribel felt an electric sensation. "What are you talking about?"

"I mean there might be things to fear that maybe don't

breathe or swim. I don't believe those tales about the lagoon, either. But the old folks here claim it's true."

"Evil spirits, I bet," Sabina said. She sounded hopeful. "Or monsters."

Tamarin had a narrow, pretty face and large, dark eyes. Her expression became stern. "Don't tell me you believe in such nonsense. Those are just stories—superstitions, our teachers call them. Come on, let's go find Luke. I sort of like that shy, coconut-head boy."

On Katt Island, "coconut head" was a term of friendly affection.

"What kind of stories?" Sabina insisted. "I believe in things that normal kids aren't supposed to believe. That's why I like it here."

There were hundreds of islands in the Bahamas, but this place was already special to the girl.

On a map, Katt Island was long and thin with only one paved road. Food was often cooked over a fire. Chickens, goats, and pigs ran wild. Along the road were ghostly looking houses and old churches.

Sabina loved that part.

Families who had lived on Katt Island for centuries came in every skin color. Their eyes were brown or green or bright blue, and no one cared. They all spoke English with the same musical accent.

The people reminded her of Cuba, where she and Maribel were from. In Havana, Santeria priests—Magic Makers, some called them—had befriended Sabina. They dressed in white clothing and sold good-luck charms. For a few pennies, the women in white could read the future in a small girl's hand.

Sabina had learned a lot about magic from them.

Unlike Floridians, the people of Katt Island took ghosts and magic spells seriously. They didn't pass in silence, focused on their phones. Here, adults and kids smiled and waved. They loved to sit on a shady porch—no blaring TV, no air-conditioned vaults—and tell spooky stories.

"Ghosts, yeah, and other things," Tamarin said as if sharing a secret. "Most places in the lagoon are safe, no matter day or night. But the old folks say there are a few spots it's best not to go near. Caves and such. Blue holes where jumbees and haunts live."

"Jumbees?" Sabina wanted to know.

The island girl pursed her lips. "Spirits of dead folks. Dragons supposedly live in those blue holes. People on this island love to gossip. *Sip-sip,* we call it. Just silliness, you ask me."

Sabina was delighted. "There's nothing silly about dragons. I'd love to see a dragon. What's a 'blue hole'?"

"Big round hole in the earth filled with water." Tamarin said this as if blue holes weren't a big deal. "Lots of 'em, these parts. How long has that Luke boy been missing?"

"Not missing," Maribel replied. "He gets lost a lot. If this wasn't an island, he could be halfway to Florida by now. We're worried he'll get in trouble. That's why we haven't told anyone."

Then she added, in a meaningful way, "Luke didn't come back for breakfast. He's got to be hungry. And it's getting close to lunchtime."

Tamarin, who was twelve and excelled in school, had a young cousin. She understood the significance. "You don't want the adults to find out until you're sure he's lost," she guessed.

Maribel checked her watch, nodding. They still had an hour before their noon meeting. But there was no time to waste. Afterward—if they found Luke—Captain Hannah was taking them to the place where they could see ocean-sized sharks from shore.

"Any idea where that coconut-head boy went?" Tamarin asked.

Sabina pointed toward the lagoon. "His mask and fins are missing, so he's probably swimming around back there. Who are these old folks? They might know if he's in danger or not."

"That boy's up to his knees in mud, more likely," Tamarin replied. "The tide's gone out. Nobody wanders around that lagoon at low tide. Not locals, anyway. It's dry as a desert, especially now. It's only six days until the Turtle Moon."

Finally, Maribel could say, "I've never heard of a turtle moon. What is it?"

"The big full moon in August," the local girl said. "High tides get higher, and low tides get lower. Practically no water at all in the lagoon. It's when those baby turtles are supposed to hatch." She thought for a moment. "You know, I bet that silly boy's already back at the hotel waiting for us. Let's go check."

The hotel, owned by Tamarin's mother, was called the Dilly Tree Inn. It was unlike any hotel the Estéban sisters had seen in Cuba or Florida. Those were expensive resorts—tall with lots of windows and fancy balconies.

There was nothing fancy about the Dilly Tree. The place consisted of five small cabins on a beach that overlooked the sea. Sapodilla trees grew there, heavy with fruit. Locals called sapodillas *dilly trees*, thus the name of the hotel.

The main house had a roof of thatched palm. There was a big shaded area with tables where guests ate. Trouble was, Maribel and Sabina had yet to see any "guests" at the hotel but themselves.

Maribel was concerned.

"Why would anyone come to this poor excuse for an island?" Tamarin scoffed. "We got nothing here that tourists are interested in. No big casinos for gambling. No fancy restaurants, or even a swimming pool."

The beach had the softest, whitest sand the Estéban sisters had ever seen. It curved along the lagoon for miles. It was fringed by palms and feathery-looking pines. To the right were rocky, brambly hills. The hills sloped gradually into water that was the color of blue Kool Aid.

"Tourists don't need a swimming pool when they have this," Maribel insisted.

"That's what they expect at a real hotel," Tamarin answered. "Doesn't matter. The Dilly Tree can't stay open much longer. Mama's borrowed all the money she can. If she doesn't pay the money back by October, we'll have to close the place."

Tamarin frowned. She sounded both angry and sad when she added, "Fine with me. I'm tired of this stupid island. Lots of people are moving to Nassau because there aren't any jobs."

Nassau was the capital of the Bahamas, and the largest city.

October? Maribel thought. That was only eight weeks away. Her mind went to work on the problem. "There's got to be a way to attract tourists. We'll help. Promise. Won't we, Sabina?"

The younger sister nodded eagerly. "You can't lose the Dilly Tree Inn. Where would I stay when we come back?"

"How much money did the bank loan your mother?" Maribel was thinking about the reward given to their team, Sharks Incorporated, only a month ago. The kids weren't allowed to use the money, supposedly. But maybe they could work something out.

"Wasn't a bank," the local girl said. "It was some big company in the States. A man came to the door and talked my mother into it. He didn't mention they can take a person's land if the money's not—"

Tamarin was interrupted by the distant wail of what might have been a dog.

She held up her hand, meaning, *Stop*. At the same instant, Sabina pointed and hollered, "Hey—there's Luke!"

A hundred yards down the beach, the boy had exited a fringe of palm trees. He was waving his arms as if he needed help.

"Co' mon," Tamarin called.

All three girls sprinted to see what was wrong.

SIX

THE BANANA HOLE

Luke forgot that he'd been lost in the lagoon, and he didn't care. That was because of what he'd heard while crossing the ridge in search of the sisters.

"There's a dog trapped up there," he yelled when the girls were close enough.

He pointed to a hill in the distance. "We need a rope or a ladder, and flashlights, or . . ." Luke stopped when he noticed Tamarin. "Good, you'll know what to do. Have you ever been on that ridge before?"

"Nobody in their right mind goes up there," the local girl responded. She snuck a glance at Luke's left arm. His burn scar from the lightning strike was partially visible despite a T-shirt. Just a few swirling lines, like the leaf of a fern.

"That's no place for you to be poking around," Tamarin said. "What were you doing, hiking through that bad bush?"

"Looking for you," the boy replied. "The dog fell into some kind of hole."

"What kind?" Tamarin asked. "A little potcake Bahamas dog? Or a dog owned by a tourist?"

Luke replied, "Never heard of a potcake dog."

"The local dogs with curly tails," the girl explained. "They steal cakes from the cooking pots. Did you see the dog?"

"No. The hole was too deep. You've got holes all over this darn island. So we need to watch our step—come on."

Luke started toward the trees. The ridge was several hundred yards away. He could no longer hear the dog barking.

The Estéban sisters followed. Tamarin held back. "Y'all can't make it through that bad bush without shoes. Rocks will cut your feet to pieces. Let's gather what we need and come back."

The others realized this made sense. The girls were barefoot. Luke's rubber dive boots had been sliced by the rocks he'd had to cross.

"We'll need a cutlass, too," Tamarin added.

"A cutlass?" Sabina wondered.

Maribel understood. In her notebook, she had started a list of words that were common in the Bahamas. *Sip-sip* was gossip. *Bad bush* referred to an area covered with briars and trees. A *cutlass* was the local name for a machete: a long-bladed knife with a wooden handle.

"The word dates back to pirate times," Maribel told her sister. "There were lots of pirates here. You heard what Doc said."

"That's how this island got its name," Tamarin agreed. "Moon-wreckers, we call them. Pirates, the same thing. Captain Arthur Katt, he was a very famous moon-wrecker. Lived here when he wasn't robbing ships and taking rich folks captive. He had a great-grandson who inherited all that money. Some say he was nicer, but tough in his way."

The local girl turned to Luke. "Are you sure you heard a dog and not something else howling up there?"

She said this in a way that put a hopeful grin on Sabina's face. "Ghosts and jumbees," the girl whispered. "Let's go. I've always wanted to see a ghost."

Luke, who was used to Sabina's strange mumblings, replied, "I know a dog when I hear one. If it's not dead yet, it will be soon."

"The dog fell into a banana hole," Tamarin said.

It had been a hot, long hike to the top of the hill.

"A banana what?" Maribel asked.

"A deep hole in the rocks," the local girl explained. "Most anything will grow in them holes—especially bananas. Richest dirt on the island. Don't get too close. In the bad bush, there're caves and holes everywhere. That's why I never go into the bush unless there's a path."

Luke, who had changed into jeans and leather boots, thought, *Now she tells me.*

Here there were no paths. Tamarin had led the trio up the ridge, using a machete to clear the way. They had come to a clearing. In a circle of limestone grew huge banana plants. The leaves were shaped like canoes, and almost as long. They seemed to sprout up from inside the earth.

From somewhere below, the dog yipped for attention. "The dog's getting weak," Luke said. He turned to Tamarin. "What should we do?"

The local girl was suddenly nervous. "I've heard stories of people fallin' into banana holes. Some, they say, never find their way out. Maybe we should go back and get an adult to help."

"The holes can be that deep?" Luke asked.

"Maybe even deeper," Tamarin said. "Never been in one, so I don't know."

Maribel wore shorts and a gray hooded pullover to avoid sunburn. She stood with hands on hips, taking it all in. She had seen banana plants before, but never so thick and lush.

The spot was a beautiful, waxy green. Sprouting from the stalks were big yellow clumps of bananas. They resembled gnarled fingers on a giant's fist.

While the older children debated what to do, Sabina wandered off. Several minutes later, she returned. "People used to live on this hill," she said.

In her hand was an old bottle made of purple glass. "Through those trees, there's a rock wall and what's left of a house. A big house. Like a mansion. I think we ought to explore it. When we were in the airplane? I think it's where I saw what looked like a cemetery."

Tamarin responded, "There're old farms and cemeteries all over the island. No one bothers with 'em. Same with those old bottles. You best put it in my sack with the other trash." Gathering litter and discarded plastic had been a school project. Most kids, even during vacation, still carried a garbage sack tucked into their belt.

It was Uncle Josiah's idea, the girl had told them. She often mentioned the old man. He wasn't really her uncle, but he knew everything there was to know about Katt Island.

Luke was impatient. The dog's frightened yipping gave him goose bumps. In a backpack he had brought a flashlight, gloves, a little first-aid kit, and a coil of rope.

"I'm going down there," he said, and carried the rope to the nearest tree.

Maribel didn't like the idea, but the boy was stubborn when it came to helping animals. "Luke . . . wait. First let's tie a flashlight to the rope and lower it down. You know, at least see how deep the hole is before you decide."

Tamarin agreed, adding, "Yeah—and see *what's* down there before we do something that's not very smart."

"The farm boy?" Sabina laughed. "He does stuff that's not smart all the time. We'll use my flashlight. Stay here. I'll lean over and take a look myself."

She produced a small flashlight. It was a present from Dr. Ford.

The girl crept to the hole. She switched on the light and

gazed down. The beam was blindingly bright. It reflected off the giant leaves that blocked her view.

"Be careful," Maribel warned. "Sabina, you're getting too close."

"Darn banana leaves," the girl complained. "I can't see anything." She stepped closer and pushed a giant leaf away.

Tamarin reached to grab her elbow. "Watch yourself. Lots of times, those leaves are full of fire ants. If those ants bite you, that's what it feels like—fire. It's a terrible pain them fire ants cause."

"I know what I'm doing," Sabina insisted. She yanked her arm free.

The youngest team member took another slow, sliding step. She put one tennis shoe on the rim of the hole and leaned forward. This caused a rock beneath her foot to give way.

Suddenly, with a scream, Sabina disappeared.

SEVEN
GOLD AND THE GIRL WITH HAUNTING EYES

When her footing gave way, Sabina clawed wildly for something to grab. The flashlight went flying.

As she fell, her hands found a thick banana stalk and held tight. The plant bent with the girl's weight. It lowered her slowly, slowly down into the earth.

The flashlight had landed at the bottom of the hole. It provided light. Sabina gave another brief scream when a tornado of squeaking birds spun past her face. They exited into the sunlight above.

"Watch out for the bats!" Tamarin hollered.

Bats? In Cuba, some bats were called *vampiros*. Vampire bats!

Terrified, Sabina lost her grip on the banana stalk. She prepared herself for a painful fall. Instead the girl fell less than a foot and landed on her rump. Immediately, an animal of some sort was bouncing around on her tummy, licking her face and whining for attention.

Sabina grabbed the flashlight and saw that it was a skinny white dog. It had a curly tail and a patch of black fur around one eye. A potcake dog, Tamarin would call it.

"Sabina!" Maribel cried from above, "are you okay?"

Sabina got to her feet. She scratched the dog's ears. She probed the walls of the banana hole with the flashlight's dazzling beam.

"I hate bats!" the girl shouted. "Get me out of here."

"Are you hurt?" Maribel asked again.

The walls were gray, circular like an underground tower. They were hairy with vines, and smelled of wet moss. The bottom of the hole was wider than the opening. The opening was a wedge of sunlight eight feet above the girl's head.

Giant banana leaves made it impossible to see what was happening up there.

"I think I'm okay," Sabina hollered back, then used the light to make sure. Her T-shirt was muddy. On her wrist were a couple of fiery red welts. "Stupid fire ants," she grumbled, and slapped several more ants crawling up her sleeve.

"What about the dog?" Luke wanted to know.

"Dog?" The girl's expression changed. She responded with three sharp words in Spanish.

"Stop swearing," Maribel warned.

In English, Sabina replied, "If the farm boy liked me as much as he does animals, he wouldn't have let me fall into this stupid hole. Tamarin, are they vampire bats? Think of something before they come back."

The dog continued to demand attention. "Stop it," the girl hissed. "You're scratching my leg." She pushed the dog away. The dog rolled onto its back and wagged its curly tail. That made the girl smile. "Good doggy," she whispered in Spanish. "I bet you're hungry, aren't you?"

Luke asked, "Is the dog small enough to fit into my backpack?"

Sabina answered, "Good idea. Tie the rope to your pack and drop it down." She thought for a moment. "What about me? Both of us can't fit into your backpack."

"We'll figure it out," Tamarin called to her. "You sure you're not hurt?"

"As if anyone cares," Sabina snapped in response.

The girl waited for them to loop the backpack onto a rope and lower it. She cooed endearments and scooped up the dog. She placed the animal into the bag's main compartment, then snapped the latch.

The dog's tail stuck out from one side of the bag. Its head stuck out from the other.

"Ready," she said. "Pull—and don't forget I'm next!"

The backpack levitated upward into the canopy of giant leaves.

Sabina used the flashlight to search the bottom of the pit. It was spongy with moss. There were several old bottles. Some were made of purple glass, similar to the bottle she had found earlier. Others were made of heavy black glass, as dark as chunks of tar. There were pieces of delicate china dinner plates, too.

And something else—a metal object buried in the mud. It was black with age.

Sabina found a stick and pried the object free. She knelt. The object was the size of a clothes iron, and heavy. She scraped away some mud and saw that it looked like a small teapot. It had a handle, a lid, and a spout. The girl removed the lid and dumped out a pound of brown goop.

It wasn't a teapot, she realized. It was a small metal lamp.

It wasn't iron or brass. As a member of Sharks Incorporated, she had spent a lot of time on the water, and as every boater knows, iron rusts. Brass turns green as it ages, not black.

"Wait till you see what I found," she hooted.

"Hold your horses," Luke called. "This poor dog was about to die of thirst. She's drinking."

"Fine!" Sabina fumed.

She painted the ground with the flashlight. Something else caught her eye. The moss sparkled as if a tiny golden mirror lay beneath. The girl used the stick to scrape the object into her left hand.

"Mother of stars!" Sabina gasped in Spanish when she saw what it was. It was difficult to breathe, she was so excited.

In her hand was a coin. It was the size of an American quarter, but it wasn't a quarter. The edges were square, not round. And this coin wasn't silver. It was gold! Still as bright and shiny as the day it was made.

"Are you ready?" Luke called to her. "We're going to lower the bag again. Maybe sit on it like a swing. That should work."

Sabina's heart was pounding. She took a breath and tried to calm herself. What should she do?

A dozen thoughts rushed through the girl's head. If

Luke and the others saw the gold coin, they would tell Captain Hannah, or Doc. They might have to report the coin to island officials.

Sabina didn't want that. A lot of adults would find out. They'd come up here with all kinds of tools and claim the banana hole as their own.

Nope, the girl decided. She wasn't going to let that happen. The coin was her discovery, not theirs. Same with anything else she found down here.

"Not yet!" she answered finally. "I'll tell you when I'm ready."

The boy couldn't believe what he'd just heard. "What do you mean, 'Not yet'? Are you sure you didn't land on your head?"

Sabina ignored the insult.

She used the stick to reveal another surprising find. It appeared to be a square metal plate until she had cleaned both sides.

No . . . it was a small brass picture frame. Inside was a very old photo or drawing—the girl wasn't sure which. And the glass was too dirty for her to tell if the picture was of a child or an adult.

Maribel—who everyone thought was perfect, in Sabina's

opinion—used a motherly voice to holler, "Sweetheart, how about I come down and help you get tied into the rope? I think you should see a doctor. Like, just to be safe—but it's up to you."

"Don't need a doctor, and I'm not sweet," the girl shouted back. She was using her T-shirt to scrub the picture frame clean.

From above, banana leaves rustled. Soon Luke's backpack was dangling close to her face.

"I'll pull on the rope when I'm ready," Sabina said. "Three times. Okay? But don't rush me."

Luke wasn't much of a talker. When he did speak, it was often out of frustration. Like now. "Or you could just *tell us* you're ready. Why do you have to complicate things so much?"

The girl's face reddened. She'd never met anyone who could make her mad faster than the farm boy. Luke, with his shy eyes and extremely cool lightning scars, didn't care about her. He didn't care about anyone unless it was an animal he could sell at the fair, or a dog he could train.

"Three times, I'll pull on the rope," the girl ordered again. "Think of someone but yourself for a change."

The brass picture frame required a lot of scrubbing with

her T-shirt. The flashlight was so bright, Sabina had to dim it with her hand. Gradually, details of the picture were revealed.

"Mother of stars," she whispered again, delighted by what she'd found.

It was a very old black-and-white drawing. A portrait, really, of a beautiful young woman. Her hands were folded under her chin. The ring she wore was engraved with what looked like an angel's wings and . . . something else. Sabina couldn't make it out.

"Sister, please," Maribel begged, "tie the rope around your waist and let us pull you up."

Sabina couldn't look away from the portrait. She had never seen such a beautiful face, or more haunting dark eyes. Those eyes . . . they seemed to see into Sabina's most secret thoughts.

"I'm coming down to get you," Maribel said finally.

The younger sister was startled, as if from a dream. "No . . . don't," she responded. "I'm ready to come up. Wait until I tug on the rope."

Sabina tucked the gold coin into the pocket of her shorts. It would be okay, she decided, to show the others the strange lamp and the portrait.

But the coin was her secret to keep. For now.

EIGHT
TREASURE HUNTERS AND A HEX

"Is it my imagination, or is your sister acting even weirder than usual?" Luke asked Maribel. They had fallen behind Sabina and Tamarin, who were on the beach, almost at the Dilly Tree Inn.

The skinny potcake dog had trotted off, too. It hadn't left Sabina's side since being rescued.

Overhead, the sun was high and hot, but a nice breeze came off the sea. No boats were out there, just the wind and an empty blue horizon.

"Sabina's not weird. She's just Sabina," Maribel replied. "There's nothing strange about her being herself."

The boy seemed to accept that. Maribel, however,

sensed he was right. Sabina was hiding something. *What* she was hiding, Maribel didn't know, which was okay. People had a right to their secrets. Luke, for instance, had returned from the lagoon carrying only one swim fin. Maribel had been tempted to ask how he'd lost the other fin, but chose not to. When the time was right, maybe the boy and her sister would open up. If they didn't? That was okay, too.

Maribel had secrets of her own that she did not want revealed.

Luke asked, "You really think the picture she found is more than a hundred years old? Only Sabina could find something that strange."

Etched on the back of the brass frame was a partial date: 19-something. The last two numbers of the date would be impossible to read until the frame was cleaned.

The unusual oil lamp the girl had found also needed a good cleaning.

Maribel replied, "The woman in the portrait . . . a girl in her late teens, I'd guess. She has such unusual eyes. So beautiful. And her ring—I think it's a wedding ring. It's hard to imagine a girl as pretty as her ever growing old."

"If she's a hundred years old, she's probably dead," Luke reasoned. "And not so beautiful anymore, either. That doesn't take much imagination."

"Don't say such things," Maribel scolded. "Be respectful."

Luke sighed. There was no predicting what might upset Sabina. She was so sensitive. With Maribel, though, it was usually okay to say whatever was on his mind.

"Thought I was," the boy countered. "It's not the girl's fault she got old and died. Not mine, either."

"Sorry. I shouldn't have snapped at you," Maribel said. "It's so sad, though. A teenage girl, so long ago. It's not like any picture I've ever seen. Think we should go back and explore the banana hole? Take more lights, and a ladder?" The older sister frowned and decided, "No, the brush is too thick up there. We couldn't carry a ladder."

"We could make a rope ladder," Luke suggested. "Or just use a rope with some knots in it." A moment later, he paused and pointed. "Who are those guys?"

Ahead on the beach, two men had exited the coconut palms. They weren't islanders. They were dressed like tourists—dark shirts and slacks. They carried poles that might be hiking sticks. One of the men beckoned to Tamarin and Sabina, as if he wanted to talk.

The girls stopped. The man appeared to be interested in the beach bag on Sabina's shoulder. Why else would Sabina back away a step—then reluctantly reach into the bag and produce the old bottle she had found?

Luke's thoughts turned inward to his lightning eye. He used the circle of blue to focus on the men. He didn't like what he saw. "Those aren't hiking sticks. They're metal detectors," he said.

"What?"

"Those men are carrying metal detectors. Electronic wands, sort of, that find metal buried in the ground. They're treasure hunters, probably. I don't trust them."

Maribel had learned that Luke was usually right about such things. She set off at a jog, saying, "Let's find out."

By the time the boy caught up, they were close enough to hear one of the men say, "We're looking for antique bottles. Mind telling us where you found this?"

Sabina had handed over the bottle made of purple glass. The man wore a black polo shirt. He had a bushy red beard. His metal detector lay on the ground nearby. When he held the bottle up to the light, a bracelet on his wrist tinkled with silver horseshoes for good luck.

His friend, tall, with a cigarette dangling from his lips, was looking at the bottle, too.

Red Beard and Smoky. Those names registered in Luke's mind. The circle of blue began to flash orange, like a caution light.

"I found the bottle back there," Sabina mumbled. The skinny dog she had rescued was at her feet. Wouldn't leave her alone.

"In the water?" Red Beard asked. He had noticed Luke's dive mask, and the lone swim fin in his hand.

"Sort of," Sabina replied.

Tamarin didn't understand why the girl was lying. "Sir," she interrupted, "there're bottles like that all over this island. That's why I always carry this trash sack. To pick up litter folks throw out. Plastic mostly, but glass, too."

Red Beard looked at Tamarin as if she were a child. "This bottle could be worth four or five bucks. Come on . . . tell me exactly where you found it."

"Dollars?" Sabina asked. She sensed he was lying. The bottle was probably worth more.

"Naw, not that much," the tall man said. He flipped the butt of his cigarette away. "A buck, maybe. What else you got in that bag, little girl? Maybe we'll buy it all."

He took out a pack, used a lighter, lit another cigarette, and blew smoke out his nose.

Tamarin and Sabina exchanged looks. Both men were liars. When Red Beard reached as if to grab the bag from Sabina, she pulled away. Inside the bag, the framed portrait and the lamp made a clanking sound.

The skinny potcake dog began to growl.

The bearded man was suspicious. "That's some ferocious attack dog you got there," he said. "In that bag of yours—sounds like you found something made of metal, too. What else you got in there, little girl?"

Sabina's bad temper took control. She said something in Spanish that sounded like a threat.

It was.

Red Beard had a husky laugh. He knelt and retrieved his metal detector. His eyes moved to Luke, then Maribel. "You must be her older sister," he said.

Maribel nodded.

"Thought so. Tell your sister to be smart and let us see

what you kids found. How about it? Wouldn't you like to make some money?"

Luke saw the bearded man flick a switch on his metal detector. He also noticed a logo on the guy's black Polo shirt. A fancy design, and the words *Las Vegas Resorts*.

Tamarin stepped forward. Maybe the kids from Florida didn't need money, but she and her mother did. "Sir, the best place I know for finding old bottles is the lagoon on the other side of that hotel—Dilly Tree Inn, the hotel's called."

She spoke in the formal way islanders used when addressing tourists.

Tamarin motioned to the cabins her mother owned. They were visible through the palms near the lagoon.

"The Dilly Tree, huh?" Red Beard said. "That's a funny name."

"Named for the sapodilla fruit that grows there, sir," the local girl replied. "Food is very nice at the hotel, if you'd like some lunch and a cool drink. And we got rooms available if you gentlemen need a place to stay. Special rates, sir, this time of year. I'd help you look for bottles."

"Hire you as a guide, you mean?" Red Beard seemed to

like the idea. "We've been looking for local kids who want to make some extra cash. You interested?"

"Yes, sir," Tamarin replied. "Doing what?"

"Don't worry about that now," he replied. "Maybe we can work something out later. Did you grow up on this island?"

"My whole life," Tamarin said.

The bearded man thought for a moment. "Tell me this. If there are so many bottles in the lagoon, why were you kids looking for stuff up on that ridge? My pal and I saw where you came out. Didn't we?"

Smoky was still thinking about the hotel. "Doesn't look like much of a place to me," he said. Then, in a louder voice, he told Tamarin that they were staying on a yacht they had brought over from Miami. "It's a lot nicer than that Dilly Tree dump," he added. "Come on," he said to Red Beard. "Let's hike up the hill and see for ourselves."

"No!" Sabina said in English. "You can't." She touched her cowrie-shell necklace and glared at the men.

"Why can't we?" Red Beard asked.

"Because . . . I don't like you," Sabina replied. "You're here to steal something. I bet that's why you want Tamarin's help."

The men laughed at that. But their laughter faded when the girl added, "You're not from Miami. You're from a place called Vegas. In Spanish, *vegas* means 'meadows.' But there are no meadows where you live. It's a dirty city, nothing but desert and evil people."

Red Beard seemed to have forgotten the *Las Vegas Resorts* logo on his shirt. After a glance at his partner, he managed a nervous smile. "Some crazy imagination you got, little girl. What's that have to do with us exploring the ridge?"

The beads in Sabina's hand had gone from cool to very warm. "Because you're not welcome there. The ridge is haunted. I'll put a hex on you if you try."

"A hex? Like a magic spell?" The good-luck horseshoes on Red Beard's wrist made bell sounds. "Ha! You expect that to scare us?"

"She's hiding something," Smoky told him. "We don't need these kids. Let's go."

The bearded man replied, "Hang on a sec."

On the handle of his metal detector was an electronic box. At the other end was a round plate like a Frisbee. He touched a few buttons, then extended the plate toward Sabina's bag.

Instantly, there was a wild, warbling noise.

Maribel stepped forward. "Stay away from my sister. We'll call the police if you don't give back her bottle."

"Sure will," Tamarin said. "The constables here, they're friends of mine. I'll tell them where to find you if you hike up that ridge."

"What if I told you we own the ridge?" Red Beard said, taunting them. "And all the beachfront property, too."

The local girl remained calm. "No one owns that ridge, and they never will. If you want, sir, I'll fetch the constable, and let him decide."

The men laughed off the threat, yet handed over the bottle. They didn't waste time disappearing into the trees where they'd come from.

Sabina scolded the little dog, sputtering, "Why didn't you bite him? I would've bitten him if I was a dog! They're bad men."

Luke watched the girls and the dog start toward the hotel. That was okay. He wanted some time alone.

In silence, the boy faced the trees. He cupped his hands around his ears. He couldn't see the men, but he could hear snatches of conversation.

Red Beard said in his distinctive voice, "That brat. How

did she know we're from Las Vegas?" The next phrase was garbled. "Like a black cat, those eyes of hers."

Then the man said something about Sabina's bag. And . . . *gold?*

Yes. Something about gold.

Luke couldn't be sure he'd heard correctly. But behind his eyes, the blue circle throbbed a warning. Sabina was right about the men.

It told him something else: Sabina was being secretive for a reason.

NINE
THE DANGEROUS DRIVE
TO CAPTAIN'S PLANK

After their noon meeting, Captain Hannah arrived in a dented rental van and drove the kids south on the island's only paved road. A few miles away was a beach where she claimed they might see big sharks.

Hannah was a professional fishing guide. Together, she and Dr. Ford knew a lot about the ocean, and fishing, and boats. "Truth is, I kinda hope the sharks aren't there," the fishing guide admitted when they were underway.

"Then why are we going?" Tamarin wanted to know. She had an easygoing, confident way of speaking to adults that Maribel envied. It seemed fitting that the local girl was in the front passenger seat.

Hannah explained, "I talked to Doc last night. There's a boat out of Miami that's attracting sharks in a dangerous way. Ocean sharks from deep water. It's illegal in Florida, so the boat left Miami two days ago for Katt Island. He wants us to check it out."

The biologist, as Hannah had already told them, had been delayed, but would return in his seaplane in a day or two.

Miami? Sabina immediately thought of the men they'd met on the beach.

"Never heard of a boat like that around here, Cap'n," Tamarin said. "Big sharks, they seldom come in close to the beach."

Hannah concentrated on the road, which wasn't much wider than the van. She had a map on a piece of paper, but she seldom consulted it. Too dangerous. Driving in the Bahamas was different than in Florida. Cars traveled on the left side of the road, not the right side. There were other hazards as well. Scraggly chickens and curly-tailed dogs were a constant worry. Every little house they passed was well stocked with both.

"The yacht's clients are amateur scuba divers," Hannah explained. "They don't know much about sharks."

"Tourists, you mean?" Tamarin asked. "Wonder where they're stayin'? They sure aren't booking rooms at the Dilly Tree."

Hannah said that the tourists slept aboard the boat. They ate their meals there, too. It was a luxury yacht, supposedly. After a day or two of diving with sharks, the tourists returned to Miami or Nassau by plane or cruise ship.

"The crew cuts up fish to attract sharks," Captain Hannah continued. "When the sharks show up, the tourists go into the water and take pictures. You know, with scuba tanks and masks. It's dangerous," she added. "Bad for the area, too. Doc agrees. That's why shark-diving charters are illegal in Florida. Sharks learn to associate people with food because some of the divers feed them by hand."

Tamarin found the story hard to believe. "People pay money for something so crazy?"

"A lot of money," Hannah said. "Almost a thousand dollars a day. Some of the sharks they dive with are big enough to do real damage if they mistakenly bite someone."

"*A thousand dollars?*" The local girl had to think this through. "I'm not arguing, ma'am. But my opinion is, anything that brings money to this island is a good thing, not bad. There're few enough jobs here as it is."

The fishing guide was a tall woman with dark hair, serious in her way but quick to laugh. She accepted the comment with a *We'll see* smile.

Hannah's infant son, Izaak, was behind her, strapped into a baby seat next to Maribel and Sabina. Maribel was having fun playing peekaboo with the child.

Sabina, though, was still festering about the men who had tried to steal her bottle.

Luke sensed the girl's concern but said nothing. He sat alone in the rear seat by choice.

There were a couple of reasons. Last night, he had seen something that required some thought. On the beach behind the Dilly Tree Inn was a huge slab of limestone. A smudge rock, it was called. Every night at sunset, a fire was built on the rock. The smoke kept mosquitoes away.

After dinner, Luke had used a hose to put out the fire. That was when he'd discovered something interesting. The rock slab was pocked with craters like the surface of the moon. Stick the hose in one hole, wait a minute or two, and water would spurt out of a dozen other holes.

Was Katt Island just one giant slab of limestone? That would explain all the caves and places like the Boiling Blue Hole. Water could travel underground, from one place on the island to another. But where did the water go at low tide?

This was a mystery.

The other reason Luke had chosen the rear seat was because of Hannah's baby. The kid was crazy about Luke. It made no sense to him. Izaak cooed and spit bubbles happily when in the care of others. But if the baby heard Luke's voice, he immediately bawled for attention.

At that instant, Hannah surprised the boy by calling, "Luke—you haven't said a word the whole trip. How're you doing back there?"

Luke saw Hannah's eyes in the rearview mirror. He gave her a thumbs-up. That was all.

Sabina couldn't resist commenting. "He knows the baby will start crying if he says something. Isn't that right, farm boy? Luke hates taking care of Izaak."

"Do not!" Luke protested without thinking.

Baby Izaak gave a loud belch as if surprised. The baby's head turned, looking for Luke. He shook his tiny fists, then started crying.

Sabina was proud of herself. "See? And Izaak won't stop until Luke holds him." Cooing, she spoke to the baby in Spanish.

Luke was just starting to learn Spanish, but he recognized the phrase *pig farmer*. He had heard it often enough.

Hannah thought this was funny. "Izaak loves his cousin Luke—yes, he does. Don't worry, we're almost there." She turned the van down a sandy road. There were potholes and puddles because it had rained last night.

Trees crowded in. The road curved through coconut palms, then up a steep hill, ending at a cliff that overlooked the sea.

"I know this spot," Tamarin said. She sat forward in her seat. "Captain's Plank, it's called."

"Why?" Sabina wanted to know. "Like walking the plank in a pirate movie? We saw it from the airplane. A rock ledge that drops into the ocean."

The local girl rolled her eyes as if she didn't want to discuss it. "Just more sip-sip," she said. "Another one of them old stories folks tell."

Hannah parked, wiggled Izaak into a baby carrier, and got out.

"Let's take a look," she said.

TEN
TIGER SHARK!

Captain's Plank was a limestone cliff. It dropped straight down, a hundred feet into the sea. The cliff overlooked a purple ribbon of water that sliced through the beach into the lagoon. The water glowed like neon in the bright sunlight.

Anchored below was an expensive yacht. The yacht had a huge cabin and radar antennas. The hull was long and sleek, painted black. On deck were a dozen or so tourists wearing summer wet suits. Several had scuba tanks strapped to their backs.

None of the people, Sabina decided, resembled the men who had tried to steal her bottle. But maybe they were somewhere inside the yacht.

"Stay away from the edge of the cliff," Hannah warned the kids. "We can see just fine from here."

They were close enough to hear music coming from the yacht, but too far away to hear what was being said.

Luke was the exception. He listened and let his eyes pierce the water's surface. Far below were banks of candy-colored coral. Miniature fish schooled there. His head did a slow sweep. The beach slanted downward to an underwater cliff. Fifty feet beneath the surface was a forest of rocks and darker coral.

"See . . . they're chumming for sharks," Hannah said. She didn't bother to whisper. No need. Izaak was still fussing, with an occasional yowl.

"Give him to Luke," Sabina suggested, "or they'll hear us."

"Babies are allowed to cry," the woman said. "I think he's teething. But he might be coming down with a cold."

Maribel and Tamarin stood together, studying the expensive yacht. An anchor rope angled down from the front. A man on board was running pieces of frozen fish through a meat grinder.

"A chumsicle," Maribel said. All members of Sharks Incorporated had often used the same technique. "It's like a big frozen Popsicle, just a lot smellier. The tide's going out. It'll take chunks of fish offshore to deep water. Sharks will follow the scent to the boat."

Luke stepped forward. "Sharks are already here," he said, shielding his eyes. "Holy moly—look. There are some really big ones on their way."

The Estéban sisters trusted the boy's unusual eyesight. They followed his gaze to a shallow area called a sandbar. The sandbar was lemon-colored beneath the blue water.

A shadow sailed across the bar. The shadow resembled a torpedo, snaking up from the depths. Several more shadows followed. It was a slow parade of sharks.

Some of the sharks were longer than six feet.

Maribel whispered, "This is crazy. Please tell me those tourists aren't going into the water."

The tourist divers did. A woman who appeared to be in charge went first. She rolled into the water wearing a tangle of scuba gear. She hollered up orders to the other divers, who had assembled in a line. A couple of them carried dead fish in bags—more shark food.

One by one the divers, clutching their face masks, dropped off the back of the boat.

The tide was strong. It flowed like a river toward the sea.

The divers fought the current by hanging on to a rope. Then their swim fins slapped the surface, and they swam to the bottom as a group.

Luke had to remind himself to breathe. "Out there," he said, pointing again. "See it? That one's twice the size of all the others."

It was the largest shark the kids had ever seen.

"It's a tiger shark," Luke said when the big fish was closer.

The water was clear, tinted sky blue. He could see the scuba divers beneath the surface. The tourists were clustered together on the bottom. Bubbles from their air tanks formed an umbrella above them. They knew that sharks would soon appear.

So far, only Luke could see the metallic-looking stripes on the largest shark. Captain Hannah confirmed it. "Oh my goodness . . . you're right. A tiger shark. The thing has to be twelve feet long and weigh a thousand pounds."

"Bunch of crazy fools," Tamarin whispered.

Maribel touched Hannah's arm. "We've *got* to warn them. We could holler at the crew and tell them to get those people out of the water."

Two crewmen were visible on the boat. Neither of them

was Red Beard or Smoky. One man was still grinding up chum. The other was dozing in a chair. The men were young, shirtless. They were grooving to music, plugged into their phones

There was a third person on the boat: an older woman, perhaps more than seventy. She shot photos from atop the yacht's cabin. Luke noticed that she often glanced down at the crewmen with distrust.

For someone her age, the woman's appearance was unusual. Her wild hair was dyed green, and she wore a billowing red sundress. Her floppy hat was decorated with yellow flower blossoms.

The woman was a wealthy tourist, Sabina guessed. Not part of the dive group.

Hannah was concerned about the divers. But it was a bad idea for them to come to the surface now. "They're safer underwater," she said. "The most dangerous thing they could do is splash around on the surface, trying to get on the boat."

Sharks were excitable, as Maribel knew. The sound of a person splashing might attract them. They might mistake the vibrations for the frenzy of other sharks feeding. Picturing a possible tragedy, the girl turned away.

"What's that crazy lady doing now?" Tamarin wondered.

On the boat, the old woman had stepped over the railing to get a better view of the sharks. With one hand, she clung to a wire for balance and leaned over the water. With the other hand, she snapped away with a fancy-looking camera in an orange waterproof case. Her red dress flapped in the breeze.

"She's gonna fall." Sabina spoke in a flat tone that gave Maribel a chill. The older sister had heard this tone before. Sabina was seldom wrong.

Luke couldn't take his eyes off what was happening on the bottom. The group of divers had backed themselves into a circle. Their air bubbles thundered on the surface. They were breathing fast because they were scared.

The first school of sharks had arrived. The divers had yet to see the tiger shark. It cruised above the others, near the surface. The fish was so large, it threw a shadow on the sandy bottom like an airplane.

"What a bunch of fools," Luke muttered. "Why would they do something so stupid?"

The boy was unaware he'd spoken aloud. He was mad. Sharks didn't intentionally bite people. They ate fish. But now they were being tempted to confuse the two. The sharks were being tricked, and Luke didn't like it. If the worst happened, headlines on the Internet would read "Shark Attack!" no matter the circumstances.

Enough bad stuff had been written about sharks.

He turned to Hannah. "Can we call the police? Those guys, the two crewmen, they're not even paying attention. The old lady taking pictures doesn't trust them, either."

It was true. One man, after adjusting his earbuds, had just lit a cigarette. The other had his back to the water. He was putting away the frozen chum.

Before Captain Hannah could reply, she heard a yelping scream. They looked in time to see the woman in the red dress tumble off the cabin. She fell fifteen feet into the water below.

As a fishing guide, Hannah was trained to deal with emergencies. The instant the old woman surfaced, it was obvious that she was a poor swimmer. First, her hands found her mop of green hair. It was as if she feared her hair would float away. Then she slapped the water like a drowning puppy. The tidal current would carry the woman out to sea if someone didn't help her.

"Hey . . . hey! Man overboard!" Hannah shouted to the crewmen.

For centuries, sailors had used this phrase to declare an emergency.

Luke and the girls screamed at the men, too. The crewmen didn't hear, earbuds still plugged in. Nor had they seen the woman fall.

Baby Izaak had calmed, but resumed yowling when he heard the fear in his mother's voice.

Hannah's eyes measured the distance from the yacht to the sandbar. The bar was below the cliff, to the right. Water was shallow there. If they ran to the sandbar and formed a chain, maybe they could grab the old lady's hand as she drifted past.

But the kids would have to do it. Hannah couldn't wade into the water carrying her baby.

Maribel was a good boat captain, too. She understood Hannah's orders immediately. "Come on," she hollered, giving Tamarin and Sabina a nudge. The girls raced after her, down the side of the cliff to the sandbar.

Luke hesitated. It was because of what only he could see.

The tiger shark had heard the old lady hit the water. The huge fish had turned. It was following the woman as she battled the current that was carrying her out to sea.

ELEVEN
MARIBEL TAKES CHARGE

A path twisted down the cliff to a patch of white sand. The sand formed a shallow incline into the water.

On the way downhill, Maribel searched for something to help save the woman. There was a rotting palm frond, but it was too soggy. A tangle of blue nylon rope caught the girl's attention. A storm had washed it ashore.

She grabbed the rope and pulled. The rope ripped up several yards of sand, yet it wouldn't break free. Tamarin and Sabina tried to help, but the nylon rope remained tied to something beneath the sand.

From the water, the old lady in the red dress spotted the kids. "Over here, over here! Help me!" she screamed.

The current pulled the woman under as she waved for

attention. When she surfaced, the current pushed her faster and faster toward the sandbar.

In less than a minute, it would be too late. The old lady would cross the sandbar into deep water.

Maribel gave up on the rope. "Luke, hurry!" she yelled. The boy had just reached the bottom of the cliff. Hannah was behind him, still carrying Izaak.

"Join hands—form a chain," the fishing guide ordered.

The girls did. Maribel waded into the water first. She focused on the drowning woman. Only the woman's terrified face was visible as she drifted closer.

Tamarin went next, followed by Sabina, each girl clutching the next girl's hand. The current hammered at their legs and tried to sweep them away.

Soon Hannah joined the trio by taking Sabina's hand. The fishing guide kept one foot planted on the beach. Her eyes found the drowning woman . . . then saw something that made her order the girls, "Back up, back up! Get out of the water, now!"

Maribel saw it, too. A black shark fin, tall as a fence post, had surfaced behind the old lady. The fin glistened like black glass. Beneath the fin, a massive gray shadow appeared to nudge the woman. Then the shark veered directly at the three girls who were in water up to their knees.

"Hurry! Get out of the water now!" Hannah demanded. She pulled Sabina toward the beach. Tamarin followed, but Maribel couldn't seem to make her feet move. She couldn't take her eyes off the black fin slicing toward her legs.

"It's the tiger shark!" Luke hollered from shore.

Maribel turned to see the boy charging into the water behind her. Somehow he had managed to free the coil of blue rope. Attached to the end of the rope was a small but heavy old anchor.

"Get out of my way—move!" he yelled. Then he seemed to hurl the anchor directly at Maribel's head.

The girl ducked. The anchor soared over her, and landed atop the shark with a heavy splash. Suddenly, Maribel's legs came to life. A second eruption, much bigger, scared her toward the beach. Then she stopped.

The tiger shark was gone. Its giant tail had caused the second explosion when it darted away. But the old lady in the red dress was still there, drifting fast toward the sandbar.

"Help me—please," she managed to gasp.

From the beach, Hannah continued to order Maribel out of the water.

Never, ever had Maribel disobeyed Hannah. But she did now. She couldn't let the old woman drown without at least trying to save her.

Maribel ignored the fishing guide's worried glare and called, "Tamarin, Luke, come grab my hand." She waved them toward her, adding, "Sabina, stay on the beach with Hannah and hang on to the rope."

What Maribel would ponder later was why Tamarin, Luke, and her sister had obeyed her without hesitation. They, too, had turned a deaf ear to Captain Hannah, who was more experienced. And the only adult in charge.

TWELVE
THE RESCUE OF WINIFRED CHASE

When Luke threw the anchor, he didn't expect it to whop the shark on the dorsal fin and scare the fish away. And he certainly didn't expect Maribel to ignore Hannah and take charge of the emergency. But that happened, too.

The next thing the boy knew, he and Tamarin were in the water up to their waists, following Maribel's orders.

"Pull the anchor in—hurry," the girl urged as they all struggled with the rope. Then, when the anchor was in Luke's hands, she ordered, "Okay . . . get ready. Throw it again—but farther!"

Luke coiled some rope into his left hand. He let the

anchor dangle from his right. The timing had to be perfect, so he waited.

The drowning woman was zooming toward them as if pushed by a wave. Her red sundress was visible through the clear water. It billowed like a bright pink blossom. Suddenly, the current spun her away from the sandbar toward deeper water.

The old lady was terrified. Her eyes met Luke's—a helpless expression. And he did it: He swung the anchor and catapulted it far beyond the woman, and a few yards ahead of her. The anchor landed with a splash.

Maribel and Tamarin both shouted, "Grab the rope!" Hannah and Sabina were shouting, too.

Maybe the old lady heard them. Maybe she didn't. But nylon rope floats for a while before it sinks. She saw the bright blue coil loop into the water ahead of her. She got her arms over the rope and held tight.

Maribel hollered instructions. "Wrap it around your waist . . . don't let go!" Then she helped Tamarin and Luke hold the rope while the current swung the woman toward the sandbar. "Pull—back up and keep pulling," she ordered the other kids.

They did.

Finally, the woman managed to get to her feet. Her sodden green hair appeared to be lopsided. Red rouge dripped down her cheeks. She looked older and more fragile up close. She might have been someone's grandmother.

The old lady took a step, stumbled, and fell. Tamarin, joined by Sabina, rushed to help her into shallower water.

But not shallow enough. Luke saw a trio of shadows trailing the lady. More sharks. Not as big as the tiger shark, but big enough.

Without thinking, he charged the girls, kicking water as he ran. "Get her onto the beach," he shouted. "Get out of the water—go, go, go!"

Sabina and the lady in the sopping dress both looked at the boy like he was nuts.

"For heaven's sakes," the woman sputtered. "At least let me catch my breath first. Come here, child"—she spoke to Tamarin—"take my arm before I fall again."

Tamarin was as tall as the woman. She got the woman's bony arm around her shoulder. Sabina helped, too, unconcerned.

"Wait," the old lady insisted. "Where's my hat? I lost my hat—I loved that hat. And I lost my camera, too!"

Tamarin saw the danger next—a gray shark fin had surfaced only a few yards away. Her eyes widened. She whooped and hollered, "Ma'am, forget your dang hat! We're getting you out of here!" The local girl scooped the lady up like a sack of rice and carried her toward the beach.

Sabina, unaware of the shark, followed at a slower speed. The shark fin turned toward the youngest girl. Its tail kicked a swirl of sand and snaked after her.

"Behind you!" Luke warned.

Sabina glanced over her shoulder. She froze for a second . . . then made a yipping sound and sprinted so fast toward the beach that she appeared to be running on top of the water.

Maribel grabbed Luke's arm from behind. "Great job," she said, grinning, and pulled him toward safety. She had already recovered the coil of rope and the anchor, too.

Together, they sloshed toward the little beach.

Luke looked back to make sure they weren't being followed. He noticed something odd drifting toward them. The object resembled a bouquet of flowers. Attached was a buoyant plastic orange case.

The boy backtracked a few steps while his eyes swept the surface. Never in his life had he seen so many big sharks cruising one small area. He snatched both objects out of the water and hustled them to the beach.

Captain Hannah and the girls were there, listening to the old lady sputter her thanks. Even when excited, she had a low, commanding voice. The way she spoke reminded Sabina of an old-time movie actress.

"You people are simply fabulous—really! I don't suppose you could rustle up a towel? I must look a fright."

She made a burping sound. Embarrassed, she touched a hand to her lips. "Whoops. That was very rude. No telling how much salt water I swallowed. What about a cell phone? I want to contact my attorney about those dimwits who nearly let me drown."

Hannah steadied the woman. "Relax. Get your balance. Take a few deep breaths."

"Oh, don't worry about me, kiddo," the woman said, and managed a smile. "I've been through a lot worse in my life. If I ever step on that boat again, it will be when the police arrest the owners."

The yacht was anchored a football field away. When the woman turned to point an accusing finger, she noticed Maribel and Luke. Her face brightened. "My hat!" she exclaimed. "Is that . . . yes, my camera, too. Come here, children. First you save my life, then my favorite hat. You deserve a reward."

Maribel waited for Hannah to nod approval before they approached. Luke handed over what he had found.

The old lady checked the camera first. She swiped through the recent photos and video she'd shot, and smiled as if pleased.

"Good. All the evidence my attorney will need. The company that owns that boat will regret the day they heard my name. I know a lot more about them than they realize."

"What is your name?" Hannah asked. She had checked the woman's pulse, but she wasn't convinced a doctor wasn't needed.

"My name?" The woman was taken aback by the question. "You really don't know?"

Hannah, with a mild smile, shook her head.

"My dear," the old lady informed her, "I am Winifred Chase."

This was said as a queen might say it. She gave a slight bow when Hannah introduced herself. The lady asked about Izaak—how old was the baby? After shaking water from her hat, she positioned it atop her head at a stylish angle.

Sabina liked the old lady's theatrical behavior. And she

loved her red rouged cheeks and wild green hair, although it was darker now that it was wet. And still oddly crooked on her head.

"I bet you're famous, Ms. Chase," the girl said. "Are you rich, too?"

"Call me Winifred—or Winnie," the woman instructed, still looking at Hannah. "You really *don't* recognize my name?" She wasn't offended, just curious.

"We need to get you into some dry clothes," Hannah replied. This was a polite way of saying no, she'd never heard of the woman.

"Hmm," Winifred mused. She seemed pleased. "Well, there's no reason in the world you *should* know who I am. Why would you?" Again she looked at the sleek black yacht, saying, "Dry clothes, yes, after those dimwits bring my luggage ashore. Then I'll need the best hotel on the island. Do you live here, or are you just visiting? I'll need a guide, too. I've done a lot of reading about Katt Island."

That got Tamarin's attention. "There's a very fine hotel not far from here, ma'am. Uh . . . unless you need a swimming pool."

"Winifred, or Winnie—not *ma'am*," the woman repeated, giving Tamarin an affectionate smile. "That was very sweet, the way you picked me up and carried me to the beach. Thing is, my dear, I might look old, but my legs work just fine, thank you very much."

"You didn't see the fins, did you?" Maribel said. "She's the one who probably saved your life. Not us."

"What fins?" Winifred asked.

Hannah decided not to bring up the subject of sharks. She turned her attention to the yacht. The two crewmen had lowered a rubber boat called a dinghy. It was red with a small motor.

"Looks like they finally figured out you fell overboard," the fishing guide said. "If you'll follow us up to the cliff, I'm sure we can get their attention. We'll have them bring your luggage ashore."

Luke was the last to leave. He shielded his eyes. Soon two more men appeared from inside the yacht.

They were Red Beard and his partner, Smoky.

Luke snapped his eyelids closed, as if snapping a picture. He didn't want to forget the faces of those two men.

Behind the boy's eyes, a throbbing circle of red confirmed, *They're dangerous.*

THIRTEEN
THE MYSTERY OF THE MISSING BOOKS

Luke lugged Winifred Chase's bags to the Dilly Tree Inn's nicest cabin while Tamarin and Maribel waited in the lobby for the woman to change into dry clothes.

Sabina had slipped off alone to admire her gold coin, and to gaze at the beautiful teenager in the portrait she'd found.

It was late afternoon. Storm clouds over the sea pushed a breeze across the beach.

"Ms. Winifred won't like it here," Tamarin confided to Maribel. "Tourists seldom do. When I tell them we don't have Internet, or that our phone doesn't work if it rains, they say they'll think it over and come back. But they don't."

Maribel heard tension in her new friend's voice. She knew why. Winifred Chase, who was from New York, had tried to call her attorney from the reception area, which was walled with limestone and bamboo.

The phone was dead.

Next she'd borrowed an old cell phone owned by Tamarin's mother, Alvina Rowland. Unfortunately, it could only be used at night when the satellite signals were strong. The same was true of modern smartphones, like those carried by Doc and Hannah.

"She didn't seem to mind," Maribel said. "In fact, I heard her say the Dilly Tree is a beautiful place."

"'Charming' is how she described the hotel," Tamarin countered. "I've heard tourists say that before. What 'charming' really means is 'simple.' Not good enough for most folks."

Maribel listened patiently. The local girl was in the mood to share her feelings.

Katt Island sucked, Tamarin complained. The same with their crummy hotel. Everyone in the world seemed to have money enough to buy whatever they wanted. But not the people of Katt Island.

"It's embarrassing," Tamarin said. She was getting emotional.

Maribel understood, and shared some private thoughts of her own. She and Sabina had felt the same growing up in Cuba. Cuba was a large and beautiful island, only ninety miles from Florida, but still a very poor country.

"Sabina and I couldn't believe how rich some people were when we got to Miami. All the big houses and cars. That was almost two years ago. Money and having nice things seemed important at the time. Now, though, it doesn't seem important at all."

"Maybe that's because you have everything you need," Tamarin responded, and immediately added, "I'm sorry. That sounded mean."

Now Maribel was getting emotional. "Oh, please don't worry. I know exactly how you feel. We lived in a village outside Havana—that's Cuba's largest city. I remember the way tourists looked at us. The only dresses Sabina and I had were made out of curtains from a place where our mom worked. That feeling of being poor, not good enough to have nice things. It was, yeah, like you said. I felt ashamed."

Tamarin blinked a tear away. "You really do understand."

Maribel sniffed and smiled. "I hated the thought of strangers feeling sorry for us. After we'd lived in Florida for a while, though, I figured out that . . . well, something changed. Maybe it was me."

"You don't like being rich?"

That struck Maribel as funny. "Rich? Us? Our mom works at a restaurant, Sabina works in Doc's lab, and I do babysitting. It's sort of like you and your mom. At the end of the month, we usually have just enough money to get by."

This gave the girls a reason to share more secrets. They were laughing when Winifred Chase came into the dining room, with its tile floor and thatched roof.

"Lovely view," she commented, meaning the turquoise sea and coconut palms. "And my little cabin is perfect. So tidy and practical."

Surprised, Tamarin stood a little straighter. "Thank you, ma'am. We're very fussy about being tidy here. Mama and me—my mother, I mean—we handle most of the work ourselves. You'll never find a cleaner place."

Winifred gave a nod of satisfaction as she noted the simple chairs and tables beneath ceiling fans. "Just you and your mother take care of the whole place? Alone?"

"Just us," Tamarin said. "And Mama's friend, Uncle Josiah. He's not my real uncle, but he's there when we need him. Mama and I take turns cooking and whatever else is needed. Sometimes my little cousin does chores, too. Now that Maribel and her sister are here, they help. So does Luke."

The local girl hesitated before asking, "You don't mind us having no Internet? And the phone—might as well not have one of those, either. I'm sure sorry about that."

"Are you kidding?" Winifred said. "Kiddo, I get hundreds of e-mails a week, and my phone never stops ringing. I don't miss that one bit."

Maribel was impressed. "I've never met anyone who gets hundreds of e-mails," she said.

The woman had changed into a floral chiffon kimono that matched her Easter egg–green hair. "You have now," she responded. "And it's not as fun as you might think. Why don't you kids show me around and tell me about the place?"

They toured the kitchen. "We've got a very nice garden up the hill," Tamarin said. "Local folks raise hogs and chickens. And there is always fish and fresh conch to eat."

"I love conch salad," Winifred said. The girls were impressed when she pronounced the word correctly—"konk," not "caunch."

"This time of year, we catch land crabs, too."

The woman reacted with interest. "Land crabs?"

"Some folks think it's exciting, I guess," the girl replied, as if bored. "Crabs come out at night after a rain. Gotta take a sack and a torch. A flashlight will do, too."

In truth, Tamarin loved hunting land crabs. It really was exciting. Winifred Chase seemed to agree.

"There's certainly lots to do on this island," the woman said. "And much healthier things than playing video games. How long have you and your mother owned this, uh . . . hotel?"

The girl's jaw tightened. It was the way the lady had said *hotel*.

"Inherited the property when my father died," the local girl explained.

"Oh, I am sorry" was the response.

"No need. I was just a baby when it happened. My father's people—the Rowland family—they owned a thousand acres in the back times. A gift from the king of England—that's what I was told, anyway. Now we just got this little speck of beach."

"Someone took your land?" the old lady asked. "Or did your family sell it?"

"Don't know exactly. Some of the Rowlands were poor.

Other Rowlands were wealthy cotton growers. That was the way it was on the island. Rich and poor, folks with the same name, no matter their color."

"A thousand acres," the woman murmured. She threaded her fingers together, deep in thought.

"This whole peninsula belonged to my family," Tamarin said. "The ridge, the lagoon, everything. The land's all gone wild. No one uses it, so it doesn't matter, I guess."

Winifred sounded serious when she replied, "It matters a great deal. I'll have my attorney check into it, if I ever get him on the phone." Her tone softened. "What you call 'this little speck of beach' is magnificent, I think."

Shyly, Tamarin looked at the floor. "It was my mother's idea to open a bed-and-breakfast. Don't know why she calls it a hotel. Sorta silly, you ask me. A backways place like this."

"Backways as in backward?"

Tamarin nodded. "Up at the Starlite Restaurant, they've got satellite TV. Ms. Karen runs the restaurant. I know what the rest of the world looks like because I go there sometimes and watch the news."

"You do, huh?" Winifred Chase tried not to chuckle. "Well, kiddo, I don't think it's silly at all. Or backward."

Maribel, who hadn't said much, agreed. "A week we've

been here, and we haven't had time to get bored. There's always something interesting to do."

They had stopped in what Tamarin's mother proudly referred to as "the library." The room contained a small stone fireplace, and rattan chairs, and a wall lined with books.

The woman stared at the bookshelves and murmured, "The Rowland family. That's a very common name in the Bahamas, isn't it? Fascinating."

Tamarin didn't find it fascinating, but said, "Yes, ma'am. Some might think so."

Without turning, the woman instructed, "If we're going to be friends, you have to call me Winifred, or Winnie. Not *ma'am*. Is that understood?"

"Yes . . . Ms. Winifred," Tamarin said, and it felt okay, despite the old lady's age.

The woman wandered over to the wall of books. It was several seconds before she spoke again. "You have some real classics here. A lot of old hardbacks. And some very nice books on Katt Island history."

"All alphabetized," Tamarin said. At least their hotel had that going for it.

"Huh?" Winifred was stooped over, looking at volumes on the lower shelves.

"Alphabetical order," the girl repeated. "By author. Just like in a real library. Mama—my mother—she's very strict when it comes to our books. They have to be signed out."

"How nice," Winifred said. A moment later, she waved the girls toward the beach. "Go ahead without me, dears. I'll be along in a bit."

"You don't want to see the other cabins?" Maribel asked. "My sister and I stay in what they call the tree house. It's built on a platform in a huge tree. Luke—remember Luke? He stays next door."

The woman couldn't take her eyes off the wall of books.

"Ah, yes," she said, preoccupied. "The quiet little boy who helped save my life. Maybe later, dear. You kids run along. I feel like doing some reading."

This struck Maribel and Tamarin as odd.

It got stranger.

Later, after dinner and once the dishes were washed, Tamarin's mother wagged a private finger and led both girls into the library. "Young'uns," she said, "we got at least two books missing. Can't remember exactly the titles, but they're sure enough gone. Look here for yourselves."

On a middle shelf was an empty space.

The library was in alphabetical order. There was no doubt that two or three hardbacks were gone.

Mrs. Rowland inspected the shelf. She stepped back, saying, "Yes siree bob, two books gone." After another moment of reflection she added, "Looks to me like the author's name might'a begun with the letter C. Who could've done such a thing?"

FOURTEEN
A CHURCH PICNIC AND A SNAKE

Sabina couldn't stop thinking about the mean men who had tried to look in her bag and steal the old bottle. Red Beard and Smoky, as Luke called them.

"Are you sure you saw them on the shark-diving yacht?" she asked the boy. "They're here to steal something. I'm sure of it. They were lying about looking for old bottles. I don't think they're treasure hunters, either."

It was early Sunday morning. The kids were on a platform bolted to the trunk of a large ficus tree. Luke's cabin was on one side of the platform. The girls' cabin was on the other. Each cabin consisted of a single room with sleeping cots, screened windows, and a ceiling fan.

The Tree House, a sign at the bottom of the steps read.

Luke gave this some thought. "People don't use metal detectors to find bottles. Could be they're after something else. I got a bad feeling about those guys. Around their faces, I saw this weird . . ."

He couldn't explain the colors that sometimes flashed in his head, so he let it go.

"Me too," the girl agreed. "Like visions. No one believes me, but what I see almost always comes true. That's how I knew those mean men weren't from Miami. They're from a dirty city with lots of lights."

"Visions, sure." Luke said this as politely as he could. "Look, I'm not trying to make you mad, but you're not the only one who saw the logo on Red Beard's shirt. It was kind of cool, what you did. Pretended to read his mind, and scared him. He thinks you're a witch. I heard them talking later."

"Good." The girl's grin showed a missing front tooth—until she frowned. "What do you mean, 'pretended'? What is a 'logo'?"

"On the guy's shirt pocket," Luke said. "Are you kidding? It was right there. A fancy design with a name—a company called Las Vegas Resorts. That's out west someplace."

He watched the girl's confused reaction. She didn't remember seeing a logo—whatever that was.

Luke wasn't sure what to think. "Then how did you know?" he asked.

Sabina thought back. In her head remained the clear image of neon lights and giant hotels. The city was a dry, desert place. *Las Vegas*, in Spanish, meant "the meadows."

"A vision," she repeated sharply. "I can't explain how I know what I know. You believe me, don't you?"

Luke still suspected that she'd seen the guy's shirt. He didn't argue, though. He was eager to get going.

Sabina sat on the platform with her legs dangling over. Luke stood at the railing.

Maribel had excused herself. She was behind the cabins using the outdoor shower. Privacy was provided by a bamboo screen. But it was impossible not to hear the water running. Six feet below, it splattered the ground like rain.

For Luke, the girls had become like his sisters. Which is to say that he trusted them. Usually. Yet he sometimes found them irritating. Like now. Why did he have to wait around for a girl who was already clean to get even cleaner? One shower a day was more than enough for him.

"Why's Maribel taking so long?" the boy complained. "Go tell her to hurry up. We'll be late for church."

"I don't want to go to church," Sabina snapped. "I'd rather stay here with Winnie. I love her hair. She's gonna stay at least another night because they say a big storm's coming."

The boy grumbled something and shrugged.

"Church," the girl continued. "I have to wear a stupid starched dress. Why can't we wear shorts or jeans?"

Luke grumbled something else and added, "Wouldn't worry about it. I'm not sticking around—so hurry up."

Sabina *was* worried.

Later, that was all she could think about, sitting in the front pew of the church that Tamarin and her mother attended. What if the men had found the banana hole? What if they were there right now, stealing something that might solve the mystery of the beautiful teenager with the haunting eyes?

Maribel, sitting to Sabina's left, whispered, "Stand up. Sing. At least pretend like you're singing."

To her right, Captain Hannah nodded and opened a hymnbook.

The girl stood. She snuck a glance over her shoulder.

The church was crowded with friendly, neatly dressed people. Luke had been in the last pew, closest to the door. Now he was gone.

That pig farmer is smarter than I gave him credit for, Sabina thought.

She gritted her teeth and pretended to sing.

Afterward, the church served an outdoor lunch. Each member had brought food of some type. Tables were loaded with baked bread, bowls of rice, and stewed fish. There was conch, fried and grilled, and platters of fragrant fruit and pastries.

Sabina surprised Luke as he ate a second piece of mango pie.

"I'm going to the banana hole this afternoon," she whispered. "And you're going with me."

The boy shrugged. "Sure. As long as Captain Hannah says it's okay."

The girl shook her head. *No.* "Just us. Not even Maribel. She won't do anything without permission."

Luke said, "What makes you think I will?"

"You snuck out of church. Hannah didn't notice, but I did. You do stuff without permission all the time."

Luke didn't like the girl's confident grin. He couldn't

deny it was true, but he didn't want to get into trouble. "Nope. Not unless Maribel goes. We're supposed to be a team. And Tamarin—she knows the island better than we do. She should go, too."

Sabina huffed and sighed. "Okay. But Tamarin has choir practice later, so it'll just be the three of us."

Luke spooned up another bite of sweet mango pie. "And the dog." He looked around. "Where'd your dog go?"

"That dog's just like you," the girl answered. "No one owns him. All he cares about is food. We'll need a rope ladder. That's your job. I'll pack water and bug spray and stuff. But don't blame me if Hannah says no."

Later, Maribel surprised them both by saying, "It's Sunday, our day off, so there's no need to ask Hannah, I guess. We can do whatever we want. Let's go."

Sabina tied a rope around her waist, which was easier than making a rope ladder. She was starting down into the banana hole when Luke hollered, "Stop! Back up—slowly."

The tone of his voice scared her.

"Why?"

"A snake," he said. "A big one. See it?"

Not at first. "Where?"

"Right by your hand. *Move.*"

The girl jumped back. She'd been holding on to the limb of a banana plant. There, coiled among the leaves, was a snake that was thicker than her arm. She muttered several sharp words in Spanish.

This time, Maribel didn't warn her about swearing. She threw an arm around her sister and pulled her back another few steps.

"Oh my God!" Maribel said. "It could have bitten you."

Sabina's heart thumped against her ribs. She liked to pretend that nothing frightened her. But when she was scared, she got mad. "Stupid snake! Get a stick and I'll hit it."

Luke knew that Sabina wasn't serious. He stepped toward the hole. The snake was thick-bodied, four feet long, and it had dusty yellow eyes. Its skin was buckskin brown thatched with silver stripes.

The colors, in the dark shadows of the green leaves, made the snake almost invisible.

"So cool," the boy murmured. "Let's leave it alone. Maybe it'll go away."

"Are there poisonous snakes in the Bahamas?" Maribel wondered. Then immediately corrected herself. "Venomous, I mean."

As they'd learned from Doc, the words *venomous* and *poisonous* had different meanings. Venom was injected by venomous animals. This included lionfish, stingrays, and some types of spiders, jellyfish, and snakes.

Certain plants, if eaten or touched, were poisonous. A common example was poison ivy. There were many types of poisonous leaves, flowers, fruits, and seeds in the wild. Toadstools, similar to mushrooms, could be deadly.

Luke said, "I haven't read anything about the snakes on the island. I wouldn't hurt the thing anyway. It belongs here. We don't. Let's explore around and come back when we're sure the snake's not dangerous."

Sabina was reluctant to leave. "Can't. I've got to go down there before those men find this place. Do you think they've been here?"

Maribel took her eyes off the snake long enough to consider. There was no modern trash of the sort treasure hunters might discard. And if adults had searched the hole, wouldn't they have hacked down the banana plants first?

"Except for us," she said, "I don't think anyone has been here for years."

"Tell us the truth," Luke said to Sabina. "What did you find down there? Something made of gold, wasn't it?"

The girl flexed her jaw in a stubborn way. "Stupid snake," she said again. "Come on. I'll show you the mansion where I found the old bottles."

FIFTEEN
A FORGOTTEN CEMETERY
AND A GRAVESTONE

There was no path to where Sabina had found the old bottles. She led them through a tunnel of briars to an open area.

"There it is," she said, pointing.

The "mansion" consisted of the collapsed walls of a large house. Cacti grew among the ruins. Behind the mansion, three small cottages had also crumbled into the weeds. Wooden foundations were coated with whitewashed clay. An orchard of gnarled trees still survived—huge mango and avocado trees heavy with fruit.

The sky was high and blue. No one around. Just twittering birds and the three members of Sharks Incorporated.

Sabina stepped into the mansion through the remains of a doorway. On her shoulder was the empty beach bag. "This is where I found the bottles. But I only spent a couple of minutes here. Let's spread out and explore."

Luke got the impression the girl didn't want them around.

That was okay. He and Maribel made several discoveries on their own. A stone fence had once surrounded the property. In the weeds lay a massive rusted gate. Nearby was a brass bell, green with age.

Luke tried to lift the bell. It was heavy, but he managed to turn the thing. The bell was etched with a strange symbol that included a crown, like a king might wear. And something that might have been an angel with wings.

"There had to have been a road up here," he said. "Sabina's right. Whoever owned this place must have had a lot of money."

"That pirate, you think?" Maribel wondered. "The one the island's named after. The smaller houses could've been where his crew stayed when they were hiding out."

"A plantation owner with enslaved workers, more likely," the farm boy said.

Maribel was thinking about her promise to help save

the Dilly Tree Inn. "Either way, tourists might enjoy exploring a place like this. The hotel could offer tours. Tamarin's mother only has a few weeks to pay off a loan. And if a famous pirate lived here . . ."

"Doubt it," Luke said. "Besides, Katt Island pirates were called . . ." He couldn't remember the word Tamarin had used.

"Moon-wreckers," Maribel told him. "Maybe because they attacked ships at night. That would make sense."

The boy's attention had wandered. "Hey—what are those?"

Poking out of the grass were slabs of gray sandstone. Some slabs were bigger than others.

It was a cemetery.

When Sabina heard what they had found, she hollered, "Wait for me. I'm almost done. Guess what—I know who's buried there!"

The girl had been inside the ruins of a collapsed whitewashed cottage. When she exited, her beach bag clinked with objects recently found.

Together, they explored the cemetery. There were dozens of burial markers etched with names and dates. Most had been worn smooth by time.

Maribel knelt by one of the largest gravestones. "Born December first, 1884" she read aloud. "Died . . . August thirteenth, 1910."

"The thirteenth," Sabina muttered. "Thirteen is an unlucky number. No wonder." She paused. "I hate the number thirteen."

Maribel shrugged that away. She did the math in her head before continuing, "Today is August eighth. In a few days, it'll be more than one hundred years ago that this person died. Luke, I can't make out the name. You try."

The boy squatted. He focused his inner eye. Even he couldn't decipher much more. "'Here Lies a Man of the Sea,'" he read. "'Captain . . .'" He glanced up at Maribel. "Captain Something. The name's gone."

"A sea captain!" Maribel exclaimed. "Just like Tamarin told us. Maybe he really was a moon-wrecker. Not as old as some of the famous pirates, of course. Even I know that. But he could have lived here when he wasn't robbing ships. Tourists would love this."

The boy wasn't convinced. "This is an island. There were lots of sea captains. Besides"—he touched a finger to the stone—"the letters aren't faded. Someone used a hammer—a chisel, maybe—to get rid of the dead guy's name. Like they were mad. Or didn't want anyone to know. Weird, huh?"

Sabina trotted past, saying, "That's not the grave I'm looking for." She went from marker to marker until she had viewed them all.

Her disappointment showed. "This doesn't make sense. She's missing."

"Who are you talking about?" Maribel asked.

"Not sure," Sabina said. "All I know is, her initials are LBR." The younger sister fumed for a while in silence. "She has to be here. She has to be! Wait . . . I know."

Sabina returned to the wreckage of the cottage she had just exited. Maribel followed. Luke kicked around in the weeds outside. There, beneath a gigantic mango tree, was a small white marker.

The tree had protected the stone from storms and wind. The lettering was faded but readable. Chiseled into the top of the stone was an angel. There was an ornate inscription that read:

Even in Death, Forever Young

Beneath the angel was a name and a date.

"Take a look at this," he called.

The girls came running. When Sabina saw the stone, she grasped her cowrie-shell necklace.

"I found you," she said, either laughing or teary-eyed. It was hard to tell. "LBR—the same initials. I knew I'd find you."

The name on the gravestone read:

Lucinda Bonny Rowland
Born: June 9, 1891
Died:

That part was blank.

"Rowland!" Maribel said. "That's Tamarin's last name. She has to see this. I bet they're related somehow." The older sister paused. "I wonder why they didn't add a date when the woman died?"

Sabina had disappeared into a secret place inside her head. *Even in Death, Forever Young*—those words echoed within.

"Lucinda," the girl whispered, finally. "What a beautiful name. She's trying to tell me something. Here—look. She wanted me to find this." From her beach bag, she removed a necklace made of tiny gray shells. "Just like mine," she said.

Luke was used to Sabina's strange claims. "Your beads are blue and yellow."

"Same thing, just older," the girl shot back. "They're cowrie shells. In Cuba, the women in white say that cowrie shells have secret powers. The Magic Makers would know."

She faced the ruins of the cottage. "It's almost like Lucinda led me to what used to be a fireplace. I could *feel* her hand. That's where I found the necklace—under some bricks—and this."

From the bag, she removed a small box made of black wood. Scratched into the top were the initials *L.B.R.* The box felt as heavy as iron. It had been sealed with a waxy, amber coating.

Pine sap, Luke suspected. "What's in it?"

Sabina found this irritating. "Don't rush me. I haven't opened it yet."

She started to say something else, but noticed the boy's attention suddenly shift. His hawklike expression was familiar. But she had never seen him stand on his tiptoes and sniff the air like a dog.

"What's wrong?"

Luke sniffed the air again. Maribel could smell it, too. "Cigarette smoke," she whispered.

Voices and the crunch of footsteps reached the boy's ears. There was another sound, too: the tinkling of silver good-luck charms on a bracelet.

Red Beard and Smoky, he thought.

"The guys from the shark-diving yacht, they're coming," he said. "Let's hide."

Maribel stood her ground. "We're not doing anything wrong. There's no reason to hide."

Because Sabina was scared, she got mad. "Maybe they are sneaky treasure hunters. Robbers, too," she said. "Let's spy on them. Whatever they find, they're stealing from Lucinda. We can't let that happen."

Maribel took this as an excuse to hide. In a way, she was relieved. "Just as long as you know we're not doing anything wrong. But okay."

SIXTEEN
TREASURE HUNTERS, A HEX, AND A CAVE

"Those guys didn't see the snake," Luke whispered to the girls. "But I did. Just now."

Sabina had led them to a place in the bushes with a view of the banana hole. The men, using metal detectors, had circled the area. They'd found some rusty nails and other pieces of junk. That was all.

Next they'd hacked an opening in the wall of green, canoe-shaped leaves. Red Beard was about to descend into the hole while the tall man, Smoky, held on to a coil of rope.

Maribel put her lips close to Luke's ear. "I don't see the snake, either. Where'd it go?"

The boy, who seldom smiled, was smiling. "Fell into the hole when they cut those banana stalks. I bet that's one mad snake. Watch what happens. This might be fun."

It wasn't fun for Red Beard. When the man got to the bottom of the hole, he screamed. Then he screamed again, a sort of raspy shriek. "Get me out of here," he wailed. "A snake—a big freakin' snake."

"A what?" Smoky was lighting another cigarette.

"A *snake*. There's a snake down here, you idiot. Pull—hurry up!"

Red Beard added a string of swear words that Maribel had never heard. Sabina hadn't heard the words, either. She tried to memorize them for later use.

Smoky tied the rope around his waist. He pulled and pulled.

A hand appeared among the giant leaves. Then Red Beard's head. Smoky reached to help, then made a howling sound and fell. Instead of taking his partner's hand, he'd grabbed what must have felt like a snake—but wasn't.

Luke had been watching closely.

"It bit me!" the man cried. "I'm poisoned, I'm poisoned!" He was rolling around on the ground, holding his wrist.

Red Beard, muddy and sweaty, heaved himself out of the banana hole. The rope was still knotted around his waist. He was breathing heavily.

"Stop acting like a baby!" he yelled to his friend. He thought for moment, then glanced at the banana stalks. "What bit you? What are you talking about?"

"A snake—biggest I've ever seen. It was green and slimy," Smoky moaned. "I could die!"

"Another snake?" Red Beard touched his good luck bracelet nervously. "You mean there are two snakes?"

"A dozen, how would I know?" his friend groaned. "Feels like my arm's on fire. We've got to get back to the yacht. By now those tourists are gone. We can radio for a doctor in Nassau."

Red Beard hoisted the machete they'd used for chopping like a weapon. He crouched low, as if fearing a snake attack. "Those kids got us into this mess," he grumbled bitterly. "That little girl with the braids and the missing tooth? She reminds me of a black cat. Has witch's eyes, you notice? How else could she know we're from Las Vegas?"

Red Beard prodded the leaves with the knife. "Brat. I bet she didn't find the gold here. Probably knew this place was dangerous, and tricked us into coming. That's one smart little witch we're dealing with. She put a hex on us. You heard her yourself."

Smoky, still holding his wrist, managed to sit up. "I need to get to a hospital. Hurry up before that snake bites you, too."

"*Where?*" Red Beard whirled to face the banana hole. "You see another one? This is nuts, man. Freakin' snakes are everywhere." He took a slow step back and nearly tripped over his partner.

"Help me up before I pass out," Smoky pleaded. "I'm dying. You hear me?" He reached and gave his partner's pants a sharp tug.

Red Beard mistook Smoky's fingers for the fangs of a snake. "Ouch!" he yelped. The man leaped high into the air and vaulted forward. He stumbled. He tried to catch himself, then somersaulted backward into the banana hole.

The two men were still linked by the rope. The coil of rope melted away in a blur. Smoky realized what was about to happen. He flipped onto his stomach and braced himself for impact.

The rope snapped tight. Smoky's fingers dug furrows as Red Beard's weight dragged him toward the hole.

"He-e-e-lp," he cried. "Or we're both gonna die!"

Red Beard's body landed at the bottom of the hole

with a *thunk* that echoed. The rope went slack. Smoky was stunned by his good luck. He grabbed a banana stalk and got to his feet.

From ten feet below, Red Beard bellowed, "Think I broke—I broke my toe, man! Get me out of here."

"Toe?" Smoky shouted back. "You're worried about your stupid toe? Dude, I just got bit by a snake. I need a rescue helicopter." Smoky unknotted himself. He tied the rope to the limb of the nearest tree. "Pull yourself out. I'm dizzy. We need to get back to the yacht before I faint."

He sat heavily on the ground. Red Beard battled his way out of the hole while Smoky lit another cigarette. He puffed and moaned, and massaged two big red welts on his wrist.

The kids waited in silence. They watched the men gather their gear. There was lots of yelling and swearing.

Red Beard used a nasty word before saying, "That little brat's not a kid. She's a witch, or a mind reader or something. I'm serious. Tricked us by pretending she didn't want us to come here. That magic stuff is real, man. I've known it for years."

When they left, the bearded man walked with a limp. He had to hurry to keep up with Smoky, who had begun to sob, "It hurts, it hurts—think I'm dying. Dude, I don't want to die."

The men followed an overgrown path that might have once been a road to the mansion, and disappeared.

Sabina had had to cover her mouth to keep from laughing when Red Beard fell into the banana hole. She was still grinning. "I told them to stay away because they're evil. A witch, did you hear him? He called me a witch." The girl took this as a compliment. "I'm surprised the snake didn't bite him, too."

Maribel was not smiling. "That poor man. He really might die if the snake's venomous. Maybe we should help. Or at least try to call the police from the Dilly Tree."

Luke, who hadn't taken his eyes off the men, had seen every small detail. It was safe now to speak in a normal voice. "A snake didn't bite the guy," the boy announced. "Banana stalks are slippery. Maybe it felt like a snake, but it wasn't. A bunch of fire ants bit him. I saw ants crawling all over his hand." The boy stepped out from the bushes. "I think we ought to follow those two back to their yacht."

Maribel was against the idea.

Sabina, although eager to open the strange box she'd found, couldn't resist. "They mentioned tourists," she said. "That they're gone. Maybe we'll see something they don't want us to see."

Maribel was team captain, but the vote was two to one.

SEVENTEEN
THE CAVE

The kids followed the treasure hunters from a distance. Never close enough to hear anything but the crack of branches and the rumble of their voices.

Luke was the exception.

At the bottom of the ridge, storm clouds patched the sea with streaks of green. The peninsula curved inland. The men were there, following the beach.

"Let's wait until they get around the point," Maribel suggested.

Luke already knew that Sabina was right about the tourist divers. They were gone. He'd heard Red Beard say that a cruise ship had taken them to Miami. The yacht's crew had gone ashore, too.

Even so, the boy wanted to see if big sharks were still hanging around the yacht.

"Gotta go to the bathroom," he told the girls.

"You're not the only one," Sabina complained.

Luke ignored her and wandered into the trees alone. There, among vines and shadows, was a massive wall of limestone.

The sound of flowing water drew him closer. It also increased his need to pee. When he was done, he tromped down some bushes and found a crack in the high limestone wall. A deep crack. Probably twenty feet wide, but only about three feet high.

Rushing water echoed from within. Water had worn a narrow canal through the side of the opening. It flowed like rain from a pipe.

"A cave," the boy muttered.

Not a large cave, he thought at first. The opening was oddly shaped. The image of a huge fish with its mouth open popped into his mind.

He got on his knees and peered in. Even without a flashlight he could see a high, vaulted ceiling. Shafts of limestone hung there. They reminded the boy of giant icicles. *Stalactites*, he thought they were called.

Somewhere, deep inside, a waterfall hammered unseen rocks.

Luke waited until he was accustomed to the darkness. He ducked through the opening and felt his way along a wall of wet rock. A dozen fluttering shadows screeched toward him.

They were bats. Their leathery wings fanned the space above his head, then went spiraling through the opening like smoke.

Cool, the boy thought.

Before moving to Florida, he'd belonged to 4-H, a club mostly for farm kids. He'd raised Angus steers, chickens, and several pigs. Bats were common in barn lofts. In 4-H, he'd learned that bats were mammals, not birds. They did a lot of good—ate insects and helped pollinate many types of flowers.

There was nothing scary about bats. Luke had never tried raising the strange-looking creatures, and he decided it might be fun.

Using the wall as a guide, he took a few more steps. He stopped when he saw something odd. The cavern floor appeared to be moving.

How was that possible?

The boy took a slow breath. His eyes blurred, taking in light.

The floor was alive with sea turtles. Dozens of them, crawling clumsily toward the mouth of the cave. A few were large, but most were walnut-sized. Tiny. Recently hatched.

Weird. Turtles didn't lay eggs in caves. What were dozens of baby turtles doing here?

Luke's foot kicked something soft. He knelt and found a couple of burlap sacks.

The sacks weren't rotten. Someone had been in the cave recently. But why bring a burlap sack in here?

Another odd-looking object caught his attention. It lay in a wedge of sunlight on the other side of the cavern. The object resembled a . . . yes, it looked like the foot of a giant frog.

A giant frog? That was impossible.

Luke squinted. He let the image rattle around in his brain until he figured it out.

My missing swim fin! Somehow, his Rocket fin had traveled underground all the way from the lagoon.

This was amazing.

The cave ceiling was low. He got down on his hands and knees and crawled toward his swim fin. The floor was jagged with rocks. Something—not a turtle—made a clattering, raspy sound, then went slithering away.

Was it a crab? Or another big snake?

The boy lost his nerve. He needed a flashlight. And it probably wasn't smart to explore a cave all by himself.

"Luke! Are you lost?" Sabina called from the far distance. "We're going to lose those men."

The boy hesitated, then retreated through the low limestone opening.

"I'm coming," he hollered.

On his way to the beach, Luke noticed what he should have noticed before. On the sand were thousands of featherlike tracks. The tracks had been made by baby turtles on a path that led from the cave to the sea.

Something else the boy saw were human footprints.

Some footprints were large. Some were small. But not like they belonged to young children. They were more like the footprints of someone his age.

Why, Luke wondered, would local kids come to a spooky spot like this?

EIGHTEEN
WINIFRED'S SECRET AND A SÉANCE

That evening, Mrs. Alvina Rowland shared some happy news with Maribel and her daughter, Tamarin.

"That nice lady you saved from drowning?" she said to the girls. "Ms. Winifred couldn't charter a flight 'cause the weather's supposed to turn bad. Plus, she likes it here! So she paid me for the whole week just in case. In cash!"

Tamarin and Maribel exchanged a private look. They both knew the money would help, but it wasn't enough. In a few weeks, the loan company would close the Dilly Tree Inn if they didn't receive the full payment.

"That Ms. Winifred's a fine woman," Mrs. Rowland

continued. "But, poor thing, she's got no family to look after her. Told me, her whole life she's been married to her job."

"What kind of job?" Maribel asked.

"The kind you get paid a lot for, I suppose. It's not polite to ask guests personal questions. And Ms. Winifred didn't say. She sat all alone in the library most of the day, looking at old books and typing away at a little computer."

Tamarin could sense what was coming next. Her mother was still fretting about those missing books.

"Can you girls do me a favor?" Mrs. Rowland asked. "If the right moment comes up, will you tell Ms. Winifred that she's welcome to use anything we've got? If she needs a book to read, all she's got to do is sign it out of the library. No need to just take it."

Tamarin didn't give this much thought until after Maribel had returned to her tree-house cabin. It was around nine p.m., and a storm hammered the island with rain and lightning.

The power went out, as it often did.

The girl got up and found a flashlight. When the rain slowed, she went outside to check on the guests.

It was part of her job.

The curly-tailed dog that Sabina had rescued was asleep on the porch. Its belly was full from table scraps after dinner.

Tamarin strolled down the beach to their nicest cabin. Winifred Chase was visible through the side window. The old lady had lit an oil lamp and was leafing through a book. It was a hardback book with a bright cover. Peeking into a guest's window wasn't polite, but the girl couldn't resist.

She moved closer.

The old lady wore a faded purple robe. Her hair, recently dried, was snow-cone green. It resembled finely spun cotton candy.

Tamarin crept to the window and squinted at the book. The title on the dust jacket was too small to read. But the author's name was huge. There was also a photo of the author.

It took Tamarin a second to put the two together.

In the photo, the author looked young, with luxurious auburn hair. She wore a crisp white blouse and a blazer with a fancy crest.

There was no doubt about who the author was. The

missing book had been written by the woman who was now reading it—Winifred Olivia Chase.

Tamarin gasped and crept away.

She couldn't wait to tell the kids from Florida about her discovery.

Luke was half-asleep when he heard someone tap at his cabin door.

"You okay in there?" Tamarin's voice asked.

Wind howled through the ficus tree. The floor of the cabin swayed like a hammock. By now the worst of the storm had passed, but the boy's fear of lightning had kept him awake until a few minutes ago. Stray bolts still flashed somewhere over the sea.

Luke put on shorts and a tank top and went to the door. "What do you want?" he mumbled.

"Oooh . . . sorry!" Tamarin yelped when she saw the boy. She didn't have the nerve to tell him that his face was streaked with dried toothpaste.

Apparently, Luke hadn't consulted a mirror before going to bed.

Also, for the first time, she saw the burn scar on the boy's shoulder. It resembled a lightning bolt framed by a spiderweb. Like a beautiful tattoo.

"I'm just checking on guests," the local girl said. "Talk to you later!" She spun away and hurried across the tree-house platform to the second cabin. It, too, was attached to the massive tree.

She tapped on the door, and then again but harder.

Maribel, wearing a nightshirt and white leggings, appeared. She carried a kerosene lamp. One look at Tamarin's face told her that something was wrong. "What happened?" Maribel asked. "You look like you just saw a ghost."

From inside, Sabina said in Spanish, "*Fantástico!* That's what we've been waiting for. Invite the ghost in."

Sabina was disappointed when she saw Tamarin. "Oh, it's just you. That's okay. You can help. We're having . . ." She couldn't think of the word in English.

"A séance," Maribel translated. "It's actually more of a game. With the wind and lightning, it was hard to sleep. Did you already check on Luke?"

Tamarin was too embarrassed to say the boy had looked

like a clown, there was so much toothpaste on his face. Even her discovery about Winifred Olivia Chase had slipped from her mind. She tried to recover by asking, "What's a séance?"

"It's a way of speaking to dead people. And it's not a game," Sabina said without looking up. She sat cross-legged on the floor. In the strange lamp she had found was a flickering candle. Next to the lamp, the black wooden box lay open.

It contained a faded leather diary.

Atop the diary was the portrait of the young woman with the dark, haunting eyes.

The name, Lucinda Bonny Rowland, in beautiful script, was legible on the diary's cover.

The sisters had already told Tamarin about finding the gravestone. But they hadn't mentioned the diary.

"Is it her diary?" Tamarin asked.

"Of course," Sabina replied. "Trouble is, it's written in some kind of foreign language. French, Maribel thinks. And some of the pages are too brittle to open."

"French or very old English," the older sister corrected. "The penmanship is beautiful, but it's very different from the way people write now."

"Whatever," Sabina said impatiently. "That's why we're

having a séance. We can't read the diary. Something bad happened to Lucinda, I think. That's why the electricity went out. Lucinda's ghost *willed* it to happen."

"Not really," Maribel confided to Tamarin.

"Did, too!" Sabina snapped. "How would you know? You weren't concentrating. Come on, sit down." She motioned Tamarin closer. "We have to hold hands and focus on Lucinda's portrait. I learned how to do this in Cuba. The Magic Makers—the women in white—taught me a lot of secret spells."

That much was true, Maribel knew.

Tamarin didn't want to believe in secret spells. On the other hand, it was a black, stormy night. The moon was hidden by clouds. The power might not come on until morning.

The local girl sat next to Sabina. "Talking to jumbees and haunts is up to you," she said. "But I've got something to tell you first."

She told the girls about the missing books, and what she'd seen through the cottage window. "Ms. Winifred must be famous," Tamarin finished. "Doesn't want us to know, though. Why else would she take her own book from the library, or . . . books? I only saw just the one."

"Winifred Olivia Chase," said Sabina, repeating the

name. "That's beautiful! I knew she was famous. Rich, too. I'm going to ask her to help me dye my hair." The girl pulled one of her pigtails around for inspection. "I think purple would be nice. Or bright blue—what do you think?"

Maribel took a seat on the floor. Her mind was on the nice old lady they had rescued. "I bet she came to the Bahamas to research a new book. No, wait—she was taking pictures. Why would an author need photographs for a book? Or does she write the kind of books that use pictures?"

"Maybe for a magazine story," Tamarin suggested. "Probably about diving with sharks until they almost let her drown. Now she's so mad, she'll have to write about something else. Or just go back to New York without at least mentioning our hotel."

Sounding glum, the girl added, "Mama's always wanted someone to do a story about the Dilly Tree. But why would they? There's nothing to do here. This island sucks—it's so boring."

Maribel had heard kids say the same thing about Florida. She was starting to understand an odd truth. Tamarin didn't appreciate Katt Island because it was her home. To her, sea turtles, the fish, the clear water, and the miles of white sand were boring.

Even the news about Lucinda Bonny Rowland's grave-stone hadn't interested the local girl much. Rowland was such a common island name

Tamarin's eyes no longer saw what visitors saw.

Maribel didn't think the Dilly Tree or Katt Island sucked, but she let the remark go. "Somehow," she said, "we have to convince Ms. Winifred to stay. And you're right. If she doesn't want us to know who she is, we'll have to pretend like we don't."

Maribel explained what she was thinking. They couldn't be sure the famous author had come to the Bahamas to write a story. But why not take the chance? If the lady wrote books, she could certainly write about Katt Island for a magazine or a newspaper. Maribel added, "A nice article might bring tourists here. You wouldn't lose the hotel, or have to move to Nassau."

Sabina was getting antsy. She wanted to get back to the séance. "I know how to make Winnie stay," she stated, using the author's nickname as if they were good friends.

"How?" both girls wanted to know.

"I'll show her Lucinda's diary," Sabina said. "And something else you don't know about. *Maybe.*"

"Something made of gold?" Maribel hinted.

Sabina wrinkled her nose. The coin was *her* secret. Maybe she would share the secret, maybe she wouldn't. "No more talking," she said. "You have to promise to be quiet; then maybe I will."

Sabina waited for the older girls to agree. When she continued, her voice was low and spooky. "We have to hold hands and concentrate. Stare at the candle. Let Lucinda's face float into your head, and listen to the wind. In Cuba, the women in white say that's how dead people speak to us. We can hear their voices in the wind."

The girls joined hands in a circle. The candle flame flickered on their faces. The flame sparkled from the eyes of the beautiful teenager in the portrait. It was peaceful sitting there with the wind and the rumbling storm outside.

Tamarin began to feel sleepy. The slow thumping of her heart filled a silence in her ears.

Several minutes of flickering silence passed. Maribel yawned and closed her eyes. Sabina battled the urge to yawn, too, and focused harder on the old portrait.

Outside, the wind gusted. Limbs of the great tree groaned and creaked and whined. Ten minutes passed. Soon Sabina heard the groaning as a ghostly voice saying, "I . . . AM . . . LUUUU-CIN-DAH."

"Mother of stars!" Sabina whispered. "She's outside. Did you hear her?"

Tamarin sat up and gulped. Maribel opened her eyes.

The wind rattled the cabin's thatched roof.

"I'm not kidding!" Sabina warned in a louder voice. "She's *coming*."

A wild groaning in the tree seemed to announce, "I . . . AM . . . HERE!"

Sabina looked toward the door. Her hands trembled. "Lucinda!" she hollered. "I'm your friend—don't forget that. Please . . . come in!"

The cabin door banged open. A flash of lightning brightened the room. It showed the silhouette of a person standing in the doorway.

One of the girls screamed.

Startled, the silhouette jumped backward and fell. There was a thumping noise. It sounded as if a person had skidded butt-first down the bamboo steps.

Maribel was the first to grab a flashlight. She hurried outside to the platform and looked down.

It was Luke. He was at the bottom of the steps looking up. The boy had fallen about six feet and landed in a puddle. His shirt and jeans were soaked, and his face was still streaked with toothpaste. "Are you nuts?" he yelled. "I could've broken my neck. Why'd you scream at me?"

Sabina appeared at the railing. "Oh . . . it's just him," she said. "You should've knocked. Go wash your face. You've got white goop all over you."

The boy, still angry, got to his feet. "I was about to knock when you told me to come in. So I opened the darn door. When you screamed, I fell down the stairs. You did that on purpose!"

Maribel was concerned. "Are you hurt?"

"Crazy witch-girl," the boy muttered, wiping at his face. He took a breath. "Naw, I'm fine. Just hurry up, get your shoes on. There's someone on the beach using a weird light. A torch, maybe."

"So?" Sabina responded. "Go away. We're busy talking to dead people."

She turned toward the doorway, but stopped when Luke hollered, "Fine! They're stealing turtle eggs, I think. Or baby turtles. I don't need your help."

"Yes, he does," Maribel said to her sister.

The girls hurried inside and changed clothes.

NINETEEN

A TURTLE POACHER
OR A GHOST?

Maribel and Luke led the way to the beach. They carried flashlights but didn't use them. Soon their eyes got used to the darkness.

Wind swirled across the lagoon as they walked. Black clouds spun toward open sea. The clouds revealed a stormy moon while frogs and insects churred a singsong cry from the trees.

Far down the beach was a lone figure. A large man, Luke guessed. The man carried what appeared to be a shovel. In his other hand was a stick that blazed with flames—a torch. The torch showered sparks whenever the man stuck it in the sand.

"What's he doing?" Sabina whispered.

"Digging turtle eggs, looks like," Luke said. "Just like Doc warned us. Let's make sure before we wake up Hannah."

Tamarin was reluctant to agree. "A torch doesn't prove anything. What about those people climbing around up there in the bad bush? They got torches, too." She pointed to a hill at the edge of the lagoon. It wasn't far from the ridge where Sabina had fallen into the banana hole.

The children turned to see lights trailing up the hill through the trees. They were so far away, the torches might have been carried by ants.

"No turtle nests up there, but that's a good spot for hunting crabs," Tamarin explained. "Land crabs. They come out at night after a rain. I told you there's nothing much to do on this island."

"That's right," Maribel agreed. "She told Winifred about hunting crabs earlier."

The local girl sounded evasive when she added, "See? Luke-boy got himself all worked up about nothing. We might as well go back to the hotel—or join those folks on the hill. They wouldn't mind."

To Luke, hunting crabs at night sounded fun. If they

were land crabs, though, why was the man digging on the beach?

The boy trotted ahead to investigate. It wasn't Red Beard or Smoky. He was sure of that. It was someone bigger, older, from the way the person moved.

Luke's eyes zoomed in. Yes, it was a man. He wore a headscarf, pirate-style, over a rope of braided hair. A long, heavy coat, too, despite the warm August night.

Maybe the guy realized he had been spotted. He suddenly hefted a heavy bag and tossed the torch into the water. The torch hissed and went out. Using his shovel like a cane, the man became a shadow that glided into the trees.

"Is it illegal to hunt crabs?" Luke asked when the girls had caught up.

Tamarin was definitely nervous now. "Uh . . . no," she said. "Crabs are good to eat. We catch 'em and put them in a pen to fatten them up first." The girl hesitated. "Come on, I'll show you the path up that hill. You can try it yourselves."

"Fatten up crabs?" Sabina said. "That's just gross."

It didn't sound gross to Luke. On the farm, he'd raised several kinds of animals. It was important to feed them well before taking them to market.

"Then I wonder why that guy took off so fast," the boy said.

Maribel switched on her flashlight and continued walking. Fifty yards down the beach, she found the remains of a turtle nest. It was littered with broken eggs. They resembled Ping-Pong balls.

A little farther was another empty nest, then several more. Same thing. A lot of broken eggs scattered on the sand.

Where had all the baby turtles gone?

Sabina looked from the empty holes to the trees where the person had vanished. "He wasn't hunting crabs. He was stealing turtles when they hatched," she said, and added several sharp words in Spanish.

"No more swearing," Maribel warned. "Luke understands some of what you say."

The boy had dreaded the daily Spanish lessons with the Estéban sisters. Now, though, he was beginning to enjoy eavesdropping when he could. "She can swear all she wants," Luke replied. "That guy's weird—dressed like a pirate. And you're right, he was robbing turtles' nests. He should be arrested."

Tamarin's voice became a whisper. "Don't say things

like that. Carrying a shovel doesn't mean he's a moon-wrecker. Or a turtle thief. You must've seen something I didn't."

"Get used to it," Sabina chimed in.

"Pirate, moon-wrecker, whatever," Luke said. "He's wearing a scarf and has braided hair. A heavy coat, too, like in the movies. And he walks like he's got a bad leg. Maybe wooden, but I'm not sure."

The local girl began to back away, an anxious look on her face. "Leave the gentleman alone. He's not bothering us none."

It was odd the way she said this. Maribel wondered if the girl was trying to protect the person.

Sabina felt the same. "You know who the thief is, don't you?"

Tamarin was lost in thought. Sabina had to repeat the question.

"Not sure," the local girl said. "Could've been something else."

"Like what?"

Tamarin was slow to answer. "One of them old stories from back times. The old folks say a murdered man walks these beaches when the moon is up. An old pirate, they claim. Some believe he was killed by strangers who came here to steal turtle eggs."

"A ghost? *Perfecto*," Sabina said. "Let's follow him."

"No such thing as ghosts," Tamarin replied, but her voice was shaky. "Could be he's just a nice person helping those turtles get to the water."

"Then what's he got in that sack?" Luke demanded. He was already moving fast toward the trees.

A moonlit path led beneath the limbs. It was a short path that dead-ended at the lagoon.

Luke searched the water. The surface was flat and gray beneath the moon. A shadow in the distance caught his attention. He focused and saw that it was a large man in a small rowboat.

The man was using oars, rowing fast.

The shapes of the lagoon and the mangrove islands were familiar to the boy. Unforgettable, in fact.

Yesterday morning, he had slogged past the same tiny islands when he'd heard the howling dog.

Why, Luke wondered, was the man rowing baby turtles toward the Boiling Blue Hole?

And why was he carrying a burlap sack, like the sacks Luke had found left in the cave?

Walking back to the hotel, Luke decided to tell the girls the truth about falling into the hole and getting lost.

Sabina chided him, as expected. He didn't expect Tamarin to sound so concerned.

"You coconut-head boy," the girl said. "You're lucky to be alive."

"No kidding," he responded, then realized she meant something else. "You've seen the place where the water boils up?"

"Not me," Tamarin said. "Locals stay away from there. Some folks believe something bad lives in that hole."

Luke was interested. He and Tamarin were a few steps behind the sisters. It felt okay, the two of them walking together.

"Bad? Like what?"

"You'll laugh."

"No, I won't. A snake, maybe? Or an alligator—I didn't think about alligators."

The local girl replied softly, "Close. Something with scales. Sort of a mermaid that has teeth like a dragon. That's superstition, of course. What others say, though, might be true."

Luke wanted to know more.

Tamarin explained, "I heard it from one of our teachers. She claims people have disappeared into that hole and died. But they didn't die there. Their bodies were found later, a long way from the lagoon. Like something had carried them off."

The boy could picture it, getting sucked down into the Boiling Blue Hole. The same thing had happened to his missing swim fin.

"Carried their bodies where?" he asked.

"Don't know exactly," Tamarin said. "Somewhere close to the banana hole where we found the dog. Supposedly there's a cave thereabouts. Whale Mouth Cave, it's called."

Luke stopped mid-step. "Whale Mouth? Why? Because the opening's shaped like the mouth of a big fish?"

It had to be the same cave he'd found.

"Never seen it," the girl replied. "Don't want to see it, either."

Goose bumps prickled the boy's arms. Sooner or later, he had to crawl into that cave and get his swim fin. He didn't want to go alone. "I know where it is," he said. "It's not far down the beach. We could go there now." He wasn't sleepy. They all had flashlights, and it would be nice to go with three friends he trusted.

Tamarin didn't want to admit the truth. She was scared. Since childhood, she'd heard stories about ghosts, and moon-wreckers, and creatures that lived in caves and blue holes. Her brain didn't believe the stories, but her imagination did.

After the séance, the girl wanted to avoid another haunted adventure. She also needed an excuse to change the subject. "Doubt if it's the same one. There're caves all over this island." She indicated the hill where the people with torches were still visible. "We could ask them. If they don't know where it is, I'm sure they'll let us tag along and hunt crabs."

Tamarin hoped Luke would like crabbing and forget about the cave. And the Estéban sisters would stop asking questions about the man they'd seen on the beach.

The truth was, Tamarin wasn't the only person on Katt Island whose family needed money.

TWENTY
A PLAN TO SAVE THE
DILLY TREE INN

Maribel was captain of Sharks Incorporated, not because she yelled orders, but because she was well organized.

Good captains didn't push, she had learned. They led by doing all the boring little jobs no one else wanted to bother with.

Maribel's task this morning was to keep their promise to help save the Dilly Tree Inn. "Any ideas about how to convince Ms. Winifred there are interesting things to write about on this island?" she asked the group.

They were outside on the sandy lawn. Sabina lay in a hammock strung between coconut palms. She'd been working on a new poem in her diary.

Tamarin and Luke were there, too. They had just finished the breakfast dishes. Luke was inspecting a new bandage on his index finger. "Let's invite her to go crabbing," he suggested. "But this time, everyone needs to wear gloves. Man, those crabs have some claws on them. One about took my thumb off."

He'd had a lot of fun last night chasing clattering land crabs through the brush. Maribel and Sabina had enjoyed it, too.

Tamarin had to get back to the kitchen soon. She rolled her eyes. "You daft boy. A famous writer from New York doesn't care about hunting crabs. What tourists want is a big hotel with gambling. Or a nice swimming pool with waiters to bring them drinks."

Maribel jotted Luke's idea down in a notebook anyway.

The local girl added, "A golf course would be good, too. But there's nothing like that *here*."

Tamarin wore an apron over her server's uniform. The uniform consisted of pleated shorts, sandals, and a blouse with the Dilly Tree logo on the pocket. A blue ribbon added a gloss to the girl's cinnamon-colored hair.

"I'd rather hunt crabs than golf balls any time," Luke said. A better idea flashed into his head. "Hey—why not take the old lady to the cave you told me about? The place where those dead bodies were found."

Sabina dropped her diary and sat up. "Dead people? I want to go. I bet Winnie will want to go, too."

"Ms. Winifred's got to be in her seventies," Tamarin said. "Even if she was young, no one from New York wants to search for something so creepy." The girl paused. "I don't even know where the cave is. Not exactly, anyway."

"I do," Luke said. "At least, it might be the same one."

"Doesn't matter. Winnie will help us find it," Sabina insisted. "We're both writers. Writers love caves and places where dead people are found. Is the cave haunted?"

Tamarin pretended this was a silly question. She didn't want to discuss Whale Mouth Cave. And she certainly didn't want the Sharks Incorporated kids poking around there.

Maribel, sitting at a picnic table, continued to take notes. Thirty minutes later, she had a list of activities that might convince the famous author to write an article about Katt Island and the Dilly Tree Inn.

Sabina got up and looked over her sister's shoulder. "Those ideas all sound boring," she said after scanning the list. "You need to change the wording."

Maribel was hurt but tried not to show it. She scooted over on the bench to make room for her sister. "I'm sure you can do better," she said, offering Sabina her notebook and pen.

"Of course I can," the girl said. She sat, chewed at her lip, and replaced the list of ideas line-by-line.

Crabbing was changed to *Stalking Dangerous Land Crabs*.

Find the Turtle Thief was changed to *Turtle Snatchers and a Moon-Wrecker's Ghost*.

Soon the list included:

In Search of Bones and a Haunted Cave

The Monster of the Boiling Blue Hole

Catching Sharks and Deadly Lionfish!

"Lionfish are seldom deadly," Maribel corrected her sister.

"Doc says they can be," Sabina argued. "Don't bother me. I'm almost done." She added a new idea at the end of the list and laid the pen down. The last line read:

A Gold Coin and the Mystery of a Beautiful Teenage Girl

"I knew it," Luke said when he saw the notebook. "You found a gold coin. That's why Red Beard wanted to look in your bag."

Sabina was still worried about the men. "Think they'll come after me?"

"If you found treasure, could be," Tamarin said. "Strangers often come to this island looking for moon-wreckers' gold."

"I still don't understand why pirates were called moon-wreckers," Luke said.

"'Cause that's what they did," Tamarin replied. "In back times, when a ship passed at night, they'd light torches in shallow water. Like marking a channel where there was no deep water. It was their way of tricking ships into wrecking on a reef."

The local girl paused, her eyes on Sabina. "Tell us the truth. You really found a gold coin in that banana hole? We could sure use the money. My mother and I might help you find more."

Sabina didn't want adults involved. Not until the spirit

Lucinda Bonny Rowland gave her a sign of some type. Or spoke to her in a dream.

Sometimes Sabina's dreams were so powerful, she sleep-walked.

There was no telling what could happen during one of her strange dreams.

Maribel took Captain Hannah aside and revealed what they had discovered about the famous author.

"Her books are even in the hotel's library," the girl said. "One of those book was printed ten years ago. Ms. Winifred looked younger in her picture, Tamarin says. But it's the same woman—Winifred Olivia Chase."

"We want to invite her to tag sharks this afternoon," Maribel continued. "And there are some other things she might like to try. We made a list."

"If it helps the hotel, why not?" Hannah agreed. "It might be good for her, too. That poor lady has been in the library all morning doing research."

They talked about that for a while; then the subject switched to Hannah's infant son.

"Izaak's coming down with a cold, I think," she said. "In case it gets worse, Doc's trying to find a doctor in Nassau. If the weather's okay, he should be here tomorrow. Maybe he can fly Winifred around in the seaplane."

At lunch, Winifred sat alone at a table beneath a ceiling fan. She was thin and birdlike, but she enjoyed eating. No, she *loved* to eat. That was soon obvious.

Tamarin made several trips from the kitchen with food on a tray. She served the lady fresh conch salad swimming in lime juice. Next came grilled vegetables from the garden, and a spicy dish: pigeon peas and rice.

"What's for dessert?" Winifred asked. She was pouring another cup of Mrs. Rowland's herbal tea.

"Guava duff," Tamarin replied. "Guava trees grow wild here. Mother adds fresh lemon peel and cane sugar."

The fruit pastry was served hot with icing. A dreamy expression brightened the woman's face. She took a slow bite and closed her eyes. She inhaled . . . then exhaled and made a catlike purring sound.

Hannah was at a table with Maribel. Sabina was helping

in the kitchen. Luke had wandered off with baby Izaak strapped to his chest.

"Looks like Winifred is in a good mood," the fishing guide said. "Why not show her your list and let her decide? Don't be disappointed, though, if she wants to stay in her room until the weather improves. As people get older, they're less likely to, well . . . try new things."

Maribel had copied the list onto a fresh sheet of paper. "I'll wait until she's done eating," the girl said. "But . . . I've been thinking about something."

"Oh? What's that?"

Maribel seemed troubled. "I think it's wrong to pretend we don't know that Ms. Winifred writes books. I don't like to lie. And she's probably too smart to fool anyway."

Hannah gave the girl's arm an affectionate squeeze. "Good for you, Captain Maribel," she said fondly. "I'll ask Winifred to meet us on the patio."

TWENTY-ONE
A DIAPER CHANGE AND TAGGING SHARKS

Luke paced the beach while Winifred Olivia Chase spoke with the girls on the patio. Baby Izaak, who had interrupted lunch by yowling, was asleep on the boy's chest. The kid had the sniffles. Maybe a slight fever, too.

When the meeting was over, Maribel gave Luke a private wave. Sabina stuck out her tongue, then grinned to show she was kidding.

The boy was getting used to walking around carrying a baby. The kid's stuffy nose and the occasional sneeze didn't bother him. What he wasn't getting used to was changing Izaak's diapers.

Whew! Pigs and chickens weren't nearly as bad. It wasn't

fair. Why did the baby scream when one of the Estéban sisters tried to take him?

"I guess those girls are sorta scary," Luke confided to the infant. "Look, dude, I'm tired. Was up most the night hunting crabs. Those things got great big claws that hurt."

The boy displayed his bandaged index finger as proof.

The baby's tiny fist whacked Luke on the chest. From the baby's lips came a sleepy bubble, then a sneeze. From the baby's other end came a belching sound. It was not a burp.

The boy grimaced. He sniffed. He wrinkled his sensitive nose.

Maribel recognized the expression on Luke's face. "Time for a diaper change," she said to her sister. They were walking side by side.

Sabina grinned. "I'm so glad babies don't like me. They're even more irritating than adults."

Maribel, who liked babies, said, "We'll help Luke change Izaak while we tell him the good news."

The meeting with the famous author could not have gone better.

Winifred had read through the list of activities. She'd asked a lot of questions before saying, "I'll try anything.

That's the way I've lived my life. Plus, I found a very interesting old book about Katt Island in the library."

More important, the woman *loved* the food here.

The sisters helped Tamarin with the lunch dishes while they shared the best part. "She came here to write an article for *World Traveler Magazine*. Not just about shark diving, but about a big company that's buying up a lot of land in the Bahamas."

"Why would anyone buy land here?" Tamarin asked. "It can't be worth much."

Maribel wasn't sure. The company built something called "tourist destinations," she said. Big hotels and casinos. "Ms. Winifred was in Nassau before she came here," Maribel continued. "Depending on how her visit goes, she might mention Katt Island and the Dilly Tree Inn. Wouldn't that be great?"

Tamarin's expression changed. "Did she say anything about turtle poachers?"

"No, but she probably knows," Maribel replied. "She was a newspaper reporter before she started writing books. She's helped catch criminals before."

"Winnie isn't afraid of anything," Sabina bragged while scrubbing another plate. "She's been all over the world.

Written about wars and hurricanes. I'm going to be just like her when I grow up."

Lost in thought, Tamarin grimaced. Sabina, unaware, kept gushing about the author, but Maribel knew that their friend was worried about something.

The turtle poachers, maybe?

No, the older sister decided. Why would Tamarin care about thieves?

That afternoon, the members of Sharks Incorporated impressed the famous author with their shark-tagging skills. The lagoon was so shallow and clear, a boat wasn't needed.

Not that the kids had a choice. Hannah and a local expert had taken the only boat to catch lionfish. The fish, with their stinging spines, had to be handled carefully.

"Once I show you how to avoid their stingers," Hannah had told them, "I think you'll be ready to try spearing a few lionfish. Tomorrow or the next day, maybe. When Doc gets back. For now, though, stick with small sharks."

No problem. The kids found a secluded spot at the edge

of the water. Luke cut up fish and tossed the chunks into a basin of white sand. "Shouldn't be long now," he said, wading back to shore.

Sabina baited two spinning rods. Maribel got their tagging gear ready. A beach umbrella provided shade for Winifred. The woman wore huge sunglasses but had left her favorite hat at the hotel. Instead she sported a weird-looking fishing hat with a neck flap.

"It was a gift from a friend I met during a fishing expedition," she explained. Next she unfurled a massive scarf. "Got this in Mexico. Too much sun's bad for the skin, you know. I'm very glad Hannah makes you kids wear hats and long-sleeved shirts when you're working outdoors."

The old lady sat back with a glass of iced tea. She took a sip, then wrapped the scarf around her face.

"I know, I know," she laughed. "I look like a mummy. But I'd look far worse if I didn't take care of myself."

Sabina decided this was a good time to begin a private conversation with the writer. She knelt down, so it was just the two of them. They whispered back and forth for a while.

Maribel had no idea what they discussed. And she wasn't going to ask.

Luke noticed, but didn't care. Three small, dark shadows

were snaking toward them. One delicate gray fin sliced the surface.

"Get ready," he warned Sabina. "The first fish is yours."

"I've done a lot of fishing in my time," Winifred called. "May I try to catch one, too?"

When Maribel replied, "Of course," the old lady vaulted out of her chair like a cat.

The fishing rods were in rod holders staked into the sand. Both rods bent with sudden weight. The reels shrieked. Beneath the surface, two shadows cut sizzling streaks as they tried to escape across the lagoon.

Hooting with laughter, Sabina and the old lady each landed a small shark.

"Leave your fish in the water until we're ready," Maribel instructed the woman. She measured and weighed Sabina's shark. Luke made notes on a clipboard. A tiny waterproof tag was inserted behind the shark's dorsal fin. Photos were taken. The fish was revived and released.

Maribel checked the stopwatch around her neck. "One minute, three seconds," she said, grinning. "That's a new record."

Sharks didn't look delicate, but they were easily injured. It was important to finish as fast as possible.

They went through the same procedure with the second shark. It was larger and had paler skin. When the fish had been released, Sabina and Luke reviewed the photos.

"Mine was definitely a blacktip," the girl said. "The other one, I don't know. A lemon shark, maybe?"

Luke wore a puzzled expression. "Uh . . . I'm not so sure."

"Could be a Caribbean reef shark," Maribel suggested. She wasn't sure, either.

"You mean there's actually something you children don't know about sharks?" Winifred asked, impressed by what she had just witnessed. "Hang on," she added, and hurried to get her camera. "I want to get some shots for my article. You kids are real professionals."

"Yes, we are," Sabina agreed.

Luke rebaited the hooks while Maribel admitted the truth. They weren't experts. There were many types of sharks in the Bahamas. Worldwide, there were more than four hundred different types—*species*, they were called. Some sharks were so similar in appearance that only an expert could tell them apart.

"The biologist we work for will be here soon, hopefully," Maribel said. "We'll show him the pictures. But sometimes even he's not one hundred percent sure. He taught us to never guess. There's nothing wrong with admitting that you don't know the answer."

"Good advice," Winifred said. "I've met a lot of scientists in my travels. Tell me about your biologist friend."

The lady had returned to her shady lounge chair. But she paid attention when Sabina replied, "Most people call him Doc. Or Dr. Ford. He's sort of absentminded, the way some smart adults are. I look after him because someone needs to."

"Dr. *Marion* Ford?" the famous writer asked.

Maribel was puzzled by her reaction. "You've heard of him?"

The woman started to answer, then went oddly silent. After thinking for a moment, she replied, "Actually, I spoke to several shark experts while researching my trip to the Bahamas. Dr. Ford was very helpful. When did you say he'll arrive here?"

"He went to Nassau to find a doctor because the baby is sick," Maribel replied. "He flies a small seaplane, so he's stuck there until these storms blow through. You never really know when Doc will show up."

Winifred Chase replied, "Sounds like a mysterious sort of fellow. I look forward to meeting him." She sat back, done with the subject.

Luke sensed that the old lady knew more about Doc than she was willing to admit. No matter. He had spotted another group of small shadows cruising through the clear water. "Get ready," he said. It was his turn to take the fishing rod.

During the next hour, they were too busy to talk. Seven more sharks were tagged and released. Finally, the old lady declared that she'd had enough fun for one afternoon. Also, she didn't want to miss dinner.

"Mrs. Rowland says she has something special planned. And I need a nap if we're going to catch that turtle thief tonight. Or"—the woman's tone revealed amusement—"the ghost of a murdered pirate who walks the beach. Mrs. Rowland told me the story."

Sabina and Maribel were surprised. "Tonight?" This was unexpected.

"Of course." The old lady was packing her things into a large beach bag. "We have four days until the moon is full. According to Mrs. Rowland, a full moon in August is called the Turtle Moon. That's when most of the baby turtles hatch."

"The Turtle Moon," Sabina whispered. Anytime the Turtle Moon was mentioned, it sounded romantic. The words echoed in her head like words carved into a gravestone: *Even in Death, Forever Young.*

Maribel wasn't eager to confront a bunch of thieves on a lonely beach. "Maybe we should wait until Doc and Hannah can go with us."

Winifred remained determined. "Nope, tonight and every night until the moon's full. When one's older, a person learns not to procrastinate. And tomorrow morning, we'll look for"—she smiled at Sabina—"your haunted cemetery. Or do you children have something else planned?"

Pro-cras-tuh-nate? Luke didn't know what the word meant. Hopefully it wasn't something he could be blamed for. "I'll go," he said immediately. "Then maybe we can explore that cave I found."

Sabina was excited, too.

Maribel, though, said, "We have to ask Hannah first. And Tamarin, too. It's *her* cave. We can't go without her. Besides," she added, addressing the woman, "you don't really believe in ghosts, do you?"

Winifred became serious. "Not when I was younger. But now . . . well, maybe you kids will understand one day. At my age, I'd love to believe it's possible."

TWENTY-TWO
POACHERS, LIONFISH, AND A SECRET DIARY

Captain Hannah said she couldn't allow the kids to search for a turtle thief—even if he was a ghost. Too dangerous. Besides, Izaak had a fever, and the kids couldn't go alone.

Tamarin was embarrassed that her mother had told everyone the silly old legend.

The author didn't seem to mind. "I did a lot of research before I left New York. There are poachers who go from island to island, robbing turtle nests. Not just here. Internationally. It's a multimillion-dollar business. I doubt the thief is a ghost—but who knows?"

Winifred continued, "Tonight my camera and I will take a stroll on the beach. Maybe I'll come back with evidence that will help identify the man. Find one thief, and the police might catch them all."

In a dreamy tone, she added, "But only after we eat. I couldn't bear to miss Mrs. Rowland's experimental dinner. This will be a first for me."

The woman was referring to a cooler full of lionfish that Hannah had speared that afternoon. There were a dozen packed in ice. They were odd-looking fish: brown bodies striped with gold, and adorned with a bristle of rainbow-colored spines.

The author and the kids had joined Hannah on the dock. The fishing guide was getting ready to clean her catch before taking the fillets to the kitchen.

"I've never tried lionfish, either," Hannah said. "Almost no one has. What we're hoping is, they're good to eat. Local fishermen could sell them. Restaurants might put them on menus. There would be a lot fewer lionfish to kill the local fish population."

The writer was already well informed on the subject. "Noxious exotics," she called the lionfish. "In Florida, the same thing's happening. Burmese pythons, too. Huge snakes, almost twenty feet long. They're taking over the Everglades and killing all the local wildlife."

Winifred Chase seemed to know a lot about almost everything.

This reminded Luke to look up the snake they'd seen at the banana hole. But first he watched Hannah clean a few lionfish. She wore heavy rubber gloves. She used tin snippers to clip off the venomous spines.

"You have to be really careful," she warned the kids. "Get stuck by one of those spines, it means a trip to the hospital. They're dangerous."

After the spines were gone, though, it was like filleting any normal fish.

Luke excused himself and went to the library. He selected a book called *Wildlife of the Bahamas*. The boy switched on a lamp and sat in a reading chair.

Interesting. The snake they'd seen was native to the Bahamas. A *pygmy boa*, it was called, because it was small compared to the giant boa constrictors found in other parts of the world. The snake was not venomous, he read. No threat at all to people. In fact, the pygmy boa was very shy.

Luke liked that. He'd been shy most of his life.

When frightened, the pygmy boa would curl into a tight ball and hide its head. The "shame snake," some locals called it. When very frightened, the snake had the ability to bleed from its eyes and nose, as if already injured.

Others called pygmy boas "thunder snakes" because they sometimes came out after a hard rain.

Harmless, the book said. Even so, some people hated snakes. Over decades, most of the pygmy boas had been killed for no reason. They were on the international Endangered Species list.

Good.

Luke found snakes a lot more interesting than people. Now he and the sisters had no reason not to explore the banana hole.

And, after what Red Beard and Smoky had experienced, it was unlikely they'd be back.

At dinner, lionfish, grilled on banana leaves, was a big hit. Between bites, the famous author said things such as "Incredible . . . mildest fish I've ever tasted. Chefs all over the world need to know about this."

Winifred had lived in Paris for a while. So she threw in

some French phrases having to do with what she called "cuisine."

That got Sabina's attention. "You speak French?" she asked.

Luke eavesdropped on their conversation from across the room. Yes, the woman spoke French. And yes, she'd love to see the old diary that Sabina had found.

"But just us," Sabina whispered. "A diary is private. It can't be shared. I have a picture of the girl who wrote it. A teenager. With the most beautiful eyes you've ever seen. I think something bad happened to her."

The author wanted more details. "If you don't read French, what makes you think something bad happened? What's her name? It has to be in the diary someplace."

"It is," Sabina replied. "We found her gravestone, too. But the diary, we have to keep it between us. She trusts me. All dead people trust me. Her name's Lucinda Bonny Rowland."

The woman thought the crack about dead people was funny. But then her expression changed. "Wait. Are you sure? Lucinda Bonny?"

There was a long pause while Sabina nodded.

"That's fascinating. And very unusual. There was a very

famous pirate, Captain Anne Bonny. She disappeared a long, long time ago. Some people think she might have escaped to the Bahamas."

Winifred started to talk about the pirate, but Sabina interrupted. "Lucinda's last name is Rowland. Same as Tamarin and her mother. That's the most common name on Katt Island. They don't think it's important. But I do."

The woman turned inward, thinking. Her rosy cheeks brightened as she smiled. Then she shook Sabina's hand. "You've got a deal. Bring me the diary tonight. My whole life has been a secret, kiddo, so don't worry about that."

Maybe Sabina knew what that meant. Luke did not.

Even so, the boy was starting to like the old lady. In his head, though, his lightning eye colored the woman's face a foggy gray. He saw loneliness there. The old woman pretended to be fun and fearless, but she had lost confidence for some reason.

Something about her cotton-candy hair suggested a darker feeling—an illness of some type. The boy's inner eye produced an image of the famous writer in a hospital, her head shaved. Tubes in her arm.

Was her green hair a wig? Luke remembered how crooked

her hair had looked after she'd fallen off the sleek shark-diving yacht.

Sadness dulled the boy's interest. That was enough. He helped Tamarin with the dishes, then wandered out to the water's edge. The moon was bright behind fast-moving clouds. The sea, dappled with silver waves, rolled ashore.

Minutes later, the writer appeared from the shadows. She wore baggy slacks, a jacket, and the goofy-looking fishing hat. On her shoulder was a camera.

The woman didn't notice the boy. She headed down the beach alone.

She is brave, Luke thought, *but she'll never catch the turtle thief. He's too big, and she's too old.*

Later, he was in the dining room playing some kind of dumb card game with the Estéban sisters. Winifred entered the room and proved he'd been right. But also wrong.

TWENTY-THREE
PREACHER BODDEN AND THE LOCKED GATE

"The man you saw isn't a ghost, and I don't think he's a thief," the famous author announced.

She had entered the room where the kids were playing cards. It was after nine. Tiki torches blazed on the deck. Outside, a fire smoldered on the slab of limestone to keep mosquitoes away.

"He catches baby turtles when the moon's up, then moves them to a safe place," she explained. "We'll see. Tonight I'm going with him. His boat's only big enough for two, and we have to leave right away."

The woman beckoned to someone outside. "Kids, I

want you to meet Preacher Josiah Bodden. Protector of sea turtles—or so he claims."

Sabina whispered to Maribel, "Just like in the legend. The murdered man who walks the beach."

"He's not a ghost if Winifred got pictures of him," the older sister responded.

The screen door opened. A huge old man in coveralls and a straw hat entered. He had snow-white hair, and eyes fogged by age. In his hand was a shovel. He used it as a cane.

Tamarin jumped up so fast, her chair tipped over. "Uncle Josiah," she cried. "It's you!" She turned to the kids. "I told you about him."

In a way, she had. She'd said her uncle had taught Katt Island children how to swim, and how to build boats in the traditional way. But she had never referred to him as a preacher. And she had never used his full name, Josiah Bodden.

Luke sat quietly and focused inward. He noted every small detail of the old man's appearance.

Winifred continued. "It took some convincing, but I believe his story. Turns out that Preacher Bodden sometimes works with the biologist who taught you kids how to tag sharks. I wanted you to meet him first."

She went out the door, saying, "Get acquainted while I pack a few things for the boat. It might rain tonight. And Hannah's worried about her baby, so I'll check on her, too."

The screen door closed.

Maribel gave the man a frank look. "You know Dr. Ford? If that's true, why didn't he tell us? Or tell Hannah? We came here as a group."

"Call me Preacher," Josiah replied. He pulled out a chair and straddled it. But slowly, as if his back hurt. "Or Uncle Josiah. Most kids on the island do. Isn't that right, Tamarin?"

The local girl beamed. "I'll bring us a pitcher of sweet tea," she said, and left the room.

Maribel remained firm. "You didn't answer my question."

The old man liked her spirit. When he laughed, his deep voice caused the walls to vibrate. "Doc and me, we've been friends for a while. But who knows why Doc does what he does? The man's always got his reasons. Just keeps them to himself, I reckon."

That much was true, the kids knew. The biologist was private in his way. Maribel, though, sensed the old man was leaving something out.

Preacher Bodden continued, "Doc sure enough told me about you three kids. Sharks Incorporated—yes, he did. You and your sister both came from Cuba to Florida on a raft. Now, that there takes courage."

His gaze moved to Sabina. "And you, the girl with the witchy gift. Reads minds and such. Of course, Dr. Ford, being scientific, doesn't believe it. Claims you got genius instincts. Me? I choose to believe in everything."

"I probably am a genius," Sabina replied, as if she'd known that all along. She had already fallen under the old man's spell. She concentrated on his face and attempted to communicate. Without speaking, she asked, *Did you know the dead girl, Lucinda Bonny Rowland?*

Preacher Bodden seemed to respond with the slightest of nods. Then he said, "Yes, young lady, you sure do have the witchy gift. I'd love to see that picture you found. Tamarin told me about the girl with the beautiful eyes."

Had he actually heard what she was thinking? Sabina wasn't sure. "I can get the picture now. Her diary, too. They're in the tree house, hidden under my bed."

"Oh yes indeed, there are mysteries on this island that need solving," the old man said. "But not tonight. I got a sack full of baby turtles, and the tide's changing."

"A burlap sack?" Luke asked.

The old man shrugged and tilted his head. "Hear that wind pushing a storm toward us? Sound of them waves tell me all I need to know about the weather on this island. Winifred and me gotta leave soon, or we'll be trapped in the lagoon all night."

Sabina wouldn't let the subject go. "Something bad happened to Lucinda. Is that the mystery that needs to be solved? We found the mansion where she was buried. But there's no date on her gravestone."

Preacher Josiah Bodden didn't respond. His attention shifted to Luke. "And you, the boy Doc says has eyes like an owl. Says folks don't think you're smart, but you are. Told me you don't miss a thing. And you got the ears of a hound dog. That true?"

Luke pretended to study the playing cards as if he cared about the game.

"Quiet, too." The preacher's grin showed a gold front tooth. "Tamarin says, back in the lagoon, you fell into a deep hole. The Boiling Blue Hole, we call it. And that you found a cave most locals are afraid to go into. Tell me, was the opening shaped like the mouth of a whale?"

Luke locked on to the man's face. He consulted his lightning eye within. "I believe you," the boy said finally.

"Believe what?" the man asked. "I was asking about that cave."

Luke said, "I know what you were asking. On Sanibel Island, I work in Dr. Ford's lab sometimes. I heard him mention your name to a friend of his. A nice old hippie-looking guy named Tomlinson. Called you Preacher Bodden, not Uncle Josiah. They trust you. I could tell. So I guess we can trust you, too."

"Tomlinson's a fine man," the preacher said about the biologist's best friend. "A scarecrow-looking fella." He used his hand to describe Tomlinson's long, stringy hair. "Yes, sir, I've known him even longer than Doc. Son, what's that have to do with the cave you found?"

Luke looked to Maribel for guidance. She had followed every word of their conversation, but could only shrug her shoulders. She was confused.

The boy cleared his throat. "The cave—you already know I found it. How many caves have openings shaped like the mouth of a giant fish?"

The old man's foggy eyes sparked. "Fair enough," he said. "That hole you fell into? It flows way down into the earth, then into Whale Mouth Cave. Good place to release baby turtles so the poachers can't get 'em. Did you figure that out, too?"

"I should've," Luke said. "I saw baby turtles in the cave, and lots of tracks in the sand. And I found some burlap sacks. What I can't figure out is why you don't trust us enough to tell the truth."

The old man was startled. "You callin' me a liar, son?" was his rumbling reply.

"No, sir. What I think is, you and Doc are setting a trap to catch those turtle poachers."

"That so?" the man said, but didn't deny it. "What gave you such an idea?"

The boy looked to Maribel again. "Two nights ago, we saw you—well, I saw someone—rowing a sack of turtles toward what you call the Boiling Blue Hole. Doc didn't mention he's working with you. Why else would he keep it a secret? We could help, if you'd let us."

The old man liked that. "Yes, sir, young man. You three kids are smart ones." He said this in a kindly way, then grew serious.

"But it's not about trust. It's about keeping you kids out of danger. Doc and Captain Hannah feel the same. There's some bad men got their eyes on this island—and it's not just about poaching turtles."

"What are they after?" Sabina demanded. "If you don't tell us, Doc will. He tells me everything."

Amused, Preacher Bodden got up from his chair. "Young lady, there are some things about this island that outsiders don't know. Even Doc. For instance, that mansion you found? It wasn't always a mansion."

"Had to be," the girl argued. "The house was huge. It has a rock wall around the property and a big iron gate to keep out robbers. We saw it."

The man said gently, "Did it ever cross your mind that gate might have been put there to lock people *inside* the property—not keep robbers out?"

"Well . . . no. Why lock people inside?"

"'Cause that's what the gate was used for," the old preacher said. "In the back times, a wealthy family lived there, true. But they fell on bad luck when their son died. After that, the place is where the police locked up folks we used to call 'touched in the head.' Sort of a hospital. An asylum, some said."

Maribel's voice broke. "Like . . . an insane asylum?"

Tamarin was returning with a pitcher of tea when she heard Maribel's shocked reaction. The local girl stopped in the hall and listened.

Josiah Bodden retrieved his shovel and turned to Luke. "Son, that wasn't me you saw rowing that boat. The man you saw was dressed like a pirate—isn't that what you said? A moon-wrecker, we call them here."

Luke looked at the floor and nodded. Right away, he knew that Preacher Bodden was telling the truth. He wasn't the man Luke had seen on the beach.

"If it wasn't you, who was it?" Luke asked.

Before Uncle Josiah could reply, Tamarin returned to the kitchen. She had heard the story a hundred times. She didn't want the embarrassment of hearing it again.

When the moon was up, some Katt Islanders believed, a crazy person left the cemetery and roamed the beaches to protect sea turtles.

TWENTY-FOUR
SECRETS OF A BEAUTIFUL DEAD GIRL

A tropical storm hit the next morning. For two days, it hammered Katt Island with rain and swirling wind. At night, lightning sizzled. Palm trees thrashed.

Luke had convinced himself he wasn't terrified of lightning. Just careful. When he'd been zapped three months ago, it hadn't been a direct hit. A direct hit would have killed him. Even so, the pain had been awful.

Step on a hornets' nest, then swallow hot coals. It was sort of like that. Fire had burned a hole from his hand into his brain. The boy sometimes suffered nightmares. He'd wake up unable to breathe.

No big deal.

Luke wasn't smart, or so his stepfather had told him too many times. The boy no longer believed this wholeheartedly. He was smart—in many ways. In other ways, not so much. But one thing he knew for certain: Only a fool would risk going out in a lightning storm.

So he'd spent two days hiding from the storm in his cabin. When he didn't show up for meals, one of the sisters would bang at his door, bringing him food and some news.

Luke hated being waited on, but the girls insisted.

On this Wednesday afternoon, it was Sabina who brought lunch. "Winifred is so cool," she began. "We're already good friends. She's decided to write a book that takes place in the Bahamas. She wants to include stuff from the diary I found."

Luke listened to details while the girl shook water off her raincoat and hung it outside.

The diary wasn't written in French, Sabina said. It was written in a local language called Creole. Creole was a complicated mix of French and English. Preacher Bodden spoke the language. He had been helping them translate the diary, page by slow page. "I think Winnie and Preacher Bodden like each other a lot," Sabina added. "They do everything together."

But there was a problem with the diary, the girl continued. The paper had gotten damp over the years. It would take an expert, according to Winifred Chase, to carefully dry and open the many entries made in the last half of the book.

Even so, they had already learned a lot. Sabina couldn't wait to tell Luke the story on this rainy afternoon.

The dead girl, Lucinda, had been in love with an unusual man, she explained. His name was Alistar Katt. He was a sea captain, and the great-grandson of the pirate Arthur Katt. That's why his family was the richest on the island. The young sea captain was also a talented artist. Folded into the diary were several of his drawings.

"Birds, pink flamingos," Sabina said. "All sorts of herons and wild parrots. The colors have faded because the diary's so old. And the paper isn't really paper. It's thicker, like brittle leather. That's why most of the pages are stuck together."

The girl continued, "He could have become a famous naturalist, Winifred thinks. Lucinda loved him, but her family was poor. Too poor for her to marry a sea captain from a rich family. In those days, they didn't allow it. Isn't that sad?"

The boy didn't see how *not* getting married was sad, even if the guy was a boat captain. Before her death, Luke's mother and stepfather had done nothing but argue.

Sabina had such a bad temper, though, the boy nodded as if he agreed.

The girl wasn't done. "Captain Alistar didn't care about being rich. He loved Lucinda, and cared about this island—especially sea turtles. Sailors believe turtles are good luck. So he drew pictures of turtles in all sorts of colors." She waited for an impatient moment. "Pay attention, Luke! His family was rich. He liked sea turtles. And in Lucinda's portrait, she's wearing a wedding ring. Do you understand what that might mean?"

Luke was pretty sure he did. But why make Sabina mad by guessing the sea captain had gone nuts and ended up in an insane asylum after getting married?

The legend about a dead man roaming the beach was just silly. Even an artistic sea captain couldn't rise from the grave to protect turtles.

But the boy replied, "A wedding ring, yeah, interesting. What's for lunch?"

He opened the Tupperware dish. It was raw conch salad with stewed chicken and rice. "Smells good," he added. "I don't suppose you brought some ketchup."

"Ketchup?" The girl's tone showed contempt. "No one eats ketchup on conch salad or rice. What's that have to do with poor Lucinda and the man she loved? Captain Alistar had to be the one who drew her portrait. Only an artist in love

could've created something so beautiful. You still don't get it, do you?"

Luke knew he was on risky ground. "Well," he said finally, "I don't know. Are you saying the sea captain didn't like ketchup? Maybe he never tried it."

That was enough. Sabina stomped her foot and gave him a familiar lecture. "You need to stop acting like a hermit. At least come to the dining room and eat with the rest of us. Hannah thinks Izaak might have the flu. She could use your help."

"Is the kid okay?" Luke asked. Changing diapers was no fun, but he cared about the baby.

"Ask her yourself," the girl snapped. "While you've been stuck here, we explored an old church when the rain slowed. Went back to the cemetery, too. And tonight we're playing Monopoly. Are all farm boys from Ohio afraid of a little storm?"

Normally, this would have made Luke mad. But Monopoly? If not for a month at summer school, he would have failed fifth-grade math. No way was he going to make a fool of himself by trying to count fake money and numbers on a pair of dice.

"Maybe tomorrow," he replied. "Oh—and next time,

would you mind asking Maribel to bring some mustard, too?"

"Pig farmer," the girl hissed in Spanish. She banged the door on her way out into the rain.

Later, Maribel brought his dinner. Finally, there was some good news. "The weather's supposed to clear tonight. Doc's coming by seaplane in the morning."

Luke perked up. He liked people about the same, no matter their gender—which is to say he preferred not to be around anyone. But after days of being cooped up alone, only seeing the Estéban sisters when they brought his meals, he was ready for a change.

"Really? About what time?" he asked.

Maribel looked at Luke with the fondness of an older sister. "Doc wants you to meet him in the lagoon about an hour after he lands. You'll hear his seaplane."

"Just me?"

"Hannah already told us what it's about, and she has to stay with the baby. So Ms. Winifred is driving us back to the mansion where Sabina found the dead girl's grave."

The insane asylum, Luke thought.

TWENTY-FIVE
SPEARING LIONFISH THAT ROAR

Doc, the biologist, was a wide-shouldered man who noticed details despite his wire-rimmed glasses. Quiet, too, unless there was a reason to speak.

Luke liked that. People who talked just to talk missed the natural sounds—birds, croaking frogs, the crunch of a branch—that made the world a more interesting place.

"There's a lot to be learned from silence," Doc remarked. "Especially underwater."

This was after twenty minutes of snorkeling the lagoon, just the two of them. Until then, they'd hardly spoken a word.

In the water, they had both heard an odd *boom . . . boom-boom . . . boom* sound as they swam toward a bank of yellow staghorn coral. The sound resembled the thump of a beating heart.

Luke, wearing borrowed fins, stood in the shallows and cleaned his dive mask. He'd heard many clicking, popping noises while snorkeling, but never these booming roars.

"What was that?" he asked.

"Lionfish," the biologist replied. "Friends of mine recorded them underwater for the first time a couple of months ago. The fish are probably hidden somewhere near the coral. Let's see how they react when they know we're here."

Luke was the first to spot several lionfish partially buried in the sand. Their stingers resembled colorful tufts of seagrass swaying in the tide.

The boy pointed.

The biologist wore a prescription dive mask because his vision wasn't great. He flashed the *okay* sign.

They swam closer. The underwater booming changed. It became louder, faster. They heard *boom-boom-boom-boom . . . CLICK. Boom-boom-boom-boom . . . CLICK-CLICK.*

Doc, with an outstretched hand, warned the boy to stop.

They stood and tilted their masks. Both wore protective gloves. The biologist carried a pole for spearing fish. It was sort of like a slingshot with three sharp prongs at the end.

"That has to be some sort of danger signal," Luke said. He'd been assigned to carry a large plastic tube. The tube had holes in the bottom and a spring-loaded door at the top. It was made for storing dangerous fish after they'd been shot.

"A warning, yeah," Doc said. "That would be my guess, too. Thing is, biologists aren't supposed to guess. There's no doubt that fish communicate. There's a stack of research on the subject. But why and how lionfish communicate, well . . . that'll take time to figure out."

Luke sank beneath the surface and listened for several seconds. He stood. "I don't know, Doc. They're practically roaring now. It's hard to believe it's not a warning of some type."

The biologist had an easygoing manner even when he disagreed. "Lionfish roaring an alert—that fits. I can see why you believe it. But belief is . . . well, it's an opinion. What I believe, or what you believe, doesn't mean much when it comes to science. It's all about gathering information."

He handed Luke the spear—a pole spear, it was called. "Did Hannah teach you how to use this?"

The boy nodded. "The girls and I practiced on sea-grape leaves off the beach. She told us not to spear any fish. Especially lionfish."

"Show me."

Luke slipped his hand through a stretchy, rubber wristband. The wristband was connected to a fiberglass pole that was as long as he was tall. Near the end of the pole was a rubber hand grip. He floated facedown in the shallow water, stretched the pole back as far as it could go, and fired.

The boy stood and cleared his mask. "It's sort of like shooting a bow and arrow. Except my right arm is the bow, and when I let go, the spear stays connected to the pole. Trouble is, it's sorta hard to aim."

Doc said, "You're a natural. But let me show you a couple of things. First, take a closer look at the spearhead."

It was a three-pronged spear, stainless steel. Unlike most fishhooks, the spear had no barbs.

"If there were barbs, a lionfish could get stuck on the spear. Barbs would make them hard to get off. That's why we brought this big plastic tube."

A ZooKeeper, the tube was called. It was a wide piece of PVC pipe with a hinged door at the top.

Doc demonstrated. He suggested that Luke spin the pole as he stretched the rubber wristband. "Your shot will be more accurate if the pole spins when you release it."

Next, Doc pretended to spear a fish. He retrieved the pole, then inserted the spearhead into the tube. The hinged door opened, and it immediately sealed itself when the spearhead was yanked free.

"This way there's no chance of being stung. I'm sure you figured out why we can't use a regular dive bag for lionfish."

"Their spines are venomous," Luke said. "You never want to handle them."

"Exactly—they have eighteen spines, and they all look harmless. But they're like hypodermic needles. They inject a venom similar to some of the world's deadliest snakes'. Their venom has what's called a *cytotoxic* effect on animals—people included."

"Cy-to-tox-ic," Luke repeated, trying to remember the word. Doc was one of the few adults who didn't try to dumb things down for Luke to understand. The boy was eager to please him.

Cyto referred to living cells, the biologist explained. That meant that the venom was toxic to cells. Worse, it destroyed blood cells, and seemed to attack the most delicate pain sensors in the human body.

"Some people go into shock, the sting hurts so bad. Hunting lionfish is serious business, Luke. Same with tagging sharks. Hannah says she quizzed you kids on what to do if someone gets stung by a lionfish. In your dive bag, did you pack a first-aid kit?"

"Those are the rules," Luke said. "A whistle and a waterproof flashlight, too."

"Okay," the man said. "Go through the first-aid procedure for me."

Doc and Captain Hannah were big on memorizing safety procedures. The sting of a lionfish was seldom deadly, but it was very serious. There was a long list, step by step, of what to do. A trip to a hospital was always required—and the nearest hospital was a plane flight away.

"You're gonna let me spear one?" the boy asked when he was finished.

"Not just one. You'll need enough for dinner," Doc replied. "You saw them first. Come on, let's go watch those fish in action for a while. You've got a few more things to learn before I turn you loose."

They snorkeled through a garden of rose-red coral and starry clouds of fish. Beyond was a valley of white sand. Moving across the sand were dozens of lionfish. They resembled rocks, their bodies adorned with feathery stingers.

The roaring sound had changed to a steady *boom-Boom-BOOM*. Like the drums of a marching army.

The biologist stood and waited for Luke to tilt his mask back. "Lionfish hunt in packs, like wolves. They move slowly at first, scaring all the crabs and fish toward the next coral head. Once they're trapped, the lionfish move in for the kill. Pay attention. I want you to see this for yourself."

Luke did. The army of lionfish gradually circled a panicked mass of crabs and small fish. When they attacked, it was a blur of dust and drifting bits of flesh.

The lionfish seemed to inhale and swallow every living creature in their path.

Luke got to his feet. He was upset by what he'd just witnessed. "We could've stopped them," he said. "You could've used the spear. I didn't need to see that."

"Yes, you did," Doc said, very serious. "I want you to be able to explain to Maribel and Sabina why we have to do this. It's not easy to understand. What you just saw happens thousands of times a day between here and Florida. The only way to protect the sea life that belongs here is to get rid of the invaders that do not."

"Get rid of the lionfish," Luke said softly. "Yeah, I see what you mean. This won't be easy for the sisters."

Maribel and Sabina had bad memories of having to kill chickens or a pig or a rabbit for food when they'd lived in Cuba. Now Maribel seldom ate meat. And Sabina would shoo a spider out of her path rather than kill it.

"Nature, keeping things in balance, is complicated," Doc said. "Life often is."

He handed the boy the spear. "Up to you," he said. "You're going to need at least six lionfish for dinner. Spear more, and we'll fly them up to Fernandez Bay and give some to Karen at the Starlite Restaurant. Albert's Grocery would probably take the rest. I've got a cooler in the plane."

In the plane? Luke tried not to appear too excited.

The only thing he liked better than snorkeling was cruising in the biologist's seaplane. It was like a small flying boat, blue with white wings. It had wheels for landing on runways. But it also had long, canoe-shaped pontoons for landing on water.

"I didn't know we were going flying," the boy said.

Doc replied, "For now, just concentrate on spearing a lionfish without getting stung. Are you sure it won't bother you, killing a few?"

After the slaughter Luke had just witnessed, he didn't want to sound too eager. "A few would be a good start, I guess."

A "good start" turned out to be more than enough fresh lionfish to share with the Starlite Restaurant and the local grocery stores.

Wading toward the lagoon where the seaplane was moored, Doc said, "After Fernandez Bay, I want to check out that shark-diving yacht. We don't have a lot of time. In the afternoon, I'm flying Hannah and the baby to Nassau."

"Izaak's sick enough to see a doctor?" Luke wondered. "Hannah mentioned you might have to."

Doc had to smile. "Izaak probably just has a cold. But why take chances? Besides, between you and me, I have other reasons for doing a quick search of this area. You catch on to things quick, Luke. I'm going to need your help when we're in the plane."

Luke decided it was wiser to stay silent.

The biologist was often mysterious. The man would

sometimes leave Sanibel Island and not return for days. And Doc always seemed to know more than he was willing to share.

A person can't learn anything with his mouth open, the biologist had said more than once.

That had made no sense a few months ago.

Now it did.

TWENTY-SIX
THE STING OPERATION

From the seaplane, Luke looked down. Three hundred feet below, the shark-diving yacht was anchored in the same spot.

The limestone cliff, Captain's Plank, was bronze in the morning sun.

"We don't want to get too close to the boat," Doc said. "They might get suspicious. Don't want them to pull out now. See anything?"

They both wore radio headsets. It was loud inside the plane. Luke pressed the little microphone to his mouth. "Couple of big sharks still hanging around," he said. "One might be that tiger shark. See the shadow?"

Squinting, the biologist searched. "Nope. What about those two men? The ones you call Smoky and Red Beard?"

He had come to rely on the boy's unusual eyesight. It gave Luke a good feeling to be trusted. "Don't see them. They use a rubber boat to get back and forth to the island. It's a little red dinghy with a crank-start motor. That's gone, too."

"Okay, but I'm not taking any chances," Doc said.

"What's it matter if they see us?" Luke asked.

The man shook his head and replied, "Hang on."

The plane turned sharply. They flew a few miles out to sea before Doc spoke again. "I don't want you kids taking any chances, either. Those guys are bad dudes. And the people they work for are worse. Understand?"

Luke replied, "Roger that." He was learning airplane talk. Short phrases used to avoid confusion in a noisy plane.

On the beach while cleaning the lionfish Luke had shot, Doc had already revealed a few things that he had kept secret. He and the old preacher, Josiah Bodden, had been working with the police to catch a gang of turtle poachers. The author, Winifred Chase, was helping in some way.

Luke wasn't surprised to hear this, not after finding a

burlap sack in Whale Mouth Cave. The old man, Preacher Bodden, had dropped several hints, too.

"Josiah said you figured out what we're doing," the biologist added. "Is that true? He was impressed. So am I."

"Not the part about Winifred," Luke admitted. "She says she interviewed you about sharks. It was weird, though, the way she reacted when Maribel mentioned your name. Like you were sort of famous. Or that she knew things about you, but wasn't going to say."

Doc shrugged. "Winifred's got an interesting theory about the company that owns the yacht. You kids saved her life. Ask her about her idea when we get back."

When the biologist didn't want to talk about something, it was better to move on.

Luke said, "I didn't figure it out, exactly. It was more of a guess. The old guy, Preacher Bodden, wasn't poaching turtles. He's been rescuing them. Why else would you two work together, and keep it a secret from the rest of us?"

"How did you know we're working together?"

"'Cause I asked him," Luke said. "He didn't admit it. To me, that was the same as a yes. It was the way his smile sort of changed, then he folded his arms. Like protecting a secret. You know?"

The biologist nodded his approval. "There are a lot of smart people in this world," Doc said. "People a lot smarter than me. But some are so busy being smart, they don't pay attention to the small things they see and hear. That's where you're different. Luke, I think you've earned the right to hear the rest of it."

A small group of Katt Islanders, the biologist said, had been poaching turtles. The men on the yacht were paying cash to anyone willing to break the law. They considered themselves clever—let the locals do the hard, dirty work. Once safely back in Miami, the men could make a lot of money selling the turtles on what was called the international black market.

"Then they should all be arrested," Luke said through his headset microphone. "The islanders who are helping them, too."

Doc responded in a way that suggested there was another side to the story. There weren't many jobs on Katt Island, he reminded the boy. The locals had to buy food, and pay bills and rent, just like most people in the world. "Put yourself in their place, Luke."

"But it's illegal."

"That's right."

"Are you saying the islanders have no choice but to steal turtles?"

"Nope. We all have a choice. But think about it. If you had a couple of kids who needed clothes and schoolbooks, but no job, no money . . . what would you do? I'd like to think I'd come up with a legal way to get by. But who knows?"

The world, Luke realized, really was a complicated place.

Through the plane's Plexiglas door, he scanned the ocean below. Sunlight reflected off acres of sand and coral. The water had a neon glow. He had never seen so many shades of blue. Ahead, far in the distance, he noticed an unusual-looking boat.

"What's that?" the boy asked.

"Where?"

"There." Luke pointed. "A fairly big boat. Lots of antennas. But painted a weird color. Blue-green, sort of like camouflage."

The biologist chuckled. He shook his head and remarked, "Kid . . . I wish I had your eyes. That's the boat I've been looking for, but I still don't see it." The man sat back. "Take the yoke."

"What?"

"The controls," Doc said. "It's sort of like driving a tractor, but you use your feet to turn. Take us to what you see."

Luke gripped the wheel. He placed his feet on the rudder pedals and banked the plane toward the boat. It wasn't long before Doc said, "You could be a good pilot one day. I'll take it from here."

They descended to a few hundred feet. They circled the strange-looking camouflaged craft. On deck several people waved. Some wore uniforms. Some did not.

Doc spun a dial on the radio and pressed a button. He had a brief exchange with someone aboard the boat. Lots of call letters and code phrases that sounded like gibberish to the boy.

After wagging the plane's wings, Doc said, "Take the yoke again. Head toward that cave you found."

Luke grinned. He was getting the hang of flying the little plane. "Was that a police boat?" he asked.

The biologist was busy looking behind them. "Good, they're following us," he said, and sat back.

"Why?"

Doc replied, "Because Josiah spread the word about Whale Mouth Cave. Locals rob turtle nests when the moon's up, and dump them in the lagoon where you almost drowned. Next morning, the real poachers go to the cave and gather hatchlings by the hundreds."

"Then it is a police boat," Luke said into his headset. "I was right. You and Preacher Bodden set up some sort of trap. Did Hannah tell Maribel and Sabina?"

"The fewer who know, the better," Doc said. "The only reason I'm telling you is because you already figured it out. But a trap, no. Trapping criminals is illegal. But baiting them isn't. The people on the boat following us are from a government agency. What we're trying to do is set up what they call a sting operation."

"A sting? Arrest them for poaching, you mean," the boy said. "Good. But you can trust the sisters. I guarantee it. We're a team. They'll want to help if we can."

The biologist replied with a stern look. "Get us close to that cave. We'll talk later."

Ahead was the peninsula that formed the lagoon. Cabins at the Dilly Tree Inn were visible. A mile of empty beach led to the ridge where Sabina had fallen into the banana hole. The old mansion—or asylum—was up there somewhere amid a forest of green. No houses or buildings, just wild, unused land.

The limestone cliff, Captain's Plank, now had a golden tint.

Luke turned the plane slightly to the right. "The cave's straight ahead," he said. "We won't be able to see the opening because of the palm trees."

With Doc at the controls, they circled the area until the government boat was closer. He didn't say a word until they had landed in the lagoon and the engine was off.

"Luke, I don't want you going anywhere near that cave until Hannah and I get back from our doctor's appointment in Nassau. Or the shark-diving yacht either. Understood? Maribel is officially in charge, but I'm counting on all of you kids."

"Uh . . . sure," Luke stammered. "How long will you be gone?"

"You'll know when you hear my plane land," Doc replied.

Luke was in his cabin when the blue-and-white seaplane took off again. Hannah and baby Izaak were aboard.

TWENTY-SEVEN
CHURCH SECRETS AND THE GOLD DOUBLOON

The next morning, during their beach walk, Maribel looked up from her spiral notebook. She noticed a helicopter zooming low over the water.

Sabina saw the helicopter, too. Beneath it was a fast boat with flashing blue lights.

They were speeding toward the ridge where, yesterday, the girls and Winifred had explored the cemetery again. Afterward, the author had driven them up a winding road to Katt Island's oldest church, the Old Hermitage Church.

"A police helicopter," Sabina said in Spanish. "I bet they're coming to arrest those bad men. I told you Lucinda wouldn't let anyone steal from her ever again."

The girl had gotten into the habit of speaking of Lucinda as if she were a real person. Or an actual ghost.

Luke was watching from the tree-house platform. He recognized the patrol boat's blue-green camouflage. There was a helicopter, too, which a lot of people called a "chopper." He went down the bamboo steps at a run. "The shark-diving yacht," he said to the girls. "I think that's where they're headed. I bet they're busting Red Beard and Smoky for turtle poaching."

The chopper hovered, then dropped behind the ridge. The patrol boat lagged behind. It, too, vanished into the cut where they'd seen the huge tiger shark.

"Let's go watch the cops arrest them," Sabina yelled.

Maribel had to grab her sister's arm to keep her from sprinting away. "That's more than a mile down the beach," Maribel said. "Besides, Hannah and Doc told us not to leave the property."

"Then I'll go tell Winifred," Sabina said. "She'll know what to do."

Barefoot, the girl trotted away.

The famous author wasn't in her cabin. She was on the phone in the hotel lobby. Sabina waited impatiently, then wandered into the library, where Winifred had set up an office.

The author's laptop was open on a table stacked with books. A ceiling fan rattled an antique map and some musty old papers.

Tamarin was there studying the map. Her mother stood nearby, dabbing at her eyes with a hanky. Mrs. Rowland had been emotional since last night, when Winifred and the girls had returned from the Hermitage, as Preacher Bodden called it.

The Old Hermitage Church was built on Katt Island's highest hill. The place resembled a miniature castle, long abandoned by elves. Josiah had taken Winifred there on Wednesday, when the storm had passed. Last night, a Thursday, was the woman's second trip, and she'd told the girls she knew exactly where to search.

It turned out the famous author was right.

In the church steeple, they had found the map and boxes of old documents. Preacher Bodden said it was okay if they borrowed anything that Winifred believed might help save the Dilly Tree Inn.

One of the documents proved that, more than a hundred years ago, a secret wedding had taken place at the Old Hermitage Church. Lucinda Rowland, the girl in the portrait, had married Captain Alistar Katt, the great-grandson of the wealthy pirate.

After the ceremony, a priest, Father Jerome, had signed the marriage document and made notes in the church logbook. It was dated Friday, August 13, 1910.

Lucinda and Captain Alistar had chosen the full moon in August as their wedding date. Later the same night, the artistic sea captain had been murdered by turtle poachers.

At the time, the Katt family's mansion was still part of a huge farm.

There was no record of what happened to Lucinda afterward. Her small white gravestone suggested two things: Their marriage had remained a secret. And Lucinda had died alone, long after the mansion had become an insane asylum.

Sabina had wept, too, after learning this. She had cried herself to sleep, clutching the portrait of the teenage girl with haunting eyes. It was heartbreaking. The lovers, after struggling to be together, had lost each other on the night of their wedding.

Sabina's eyes were still red when Winifred, done with her phone call, entered the library. The birdlike woman wore a pleated purple blouse and walked erect, head back, as if proud of herself.

"That was my attorney," she said. She took her seat at the table and spoke to Mrs. Rowland. "I have mostly good news. Alistar Katt was an only child. After he was murdered, Lucinda Rowland, as his wife, should have inherited the mansion and most of the property. But the captain's family refused to accept Lucinda as part of the family."

Tamarin's mother had recovered her composure. "Those were tough times back then," she said. "It's all so hard to believe."

Winifred wasn't done. "Believe it," she said, and opened an old leather-bound Bible. "I found this on the bottom shelf of your library. It contains the Rowland family tree. The entries date back many generations."

Delicately, the old lady unfolded four paper panels. Written in ornate ink were dozens of names.

"This proves that Lucinda Rowland and your daughter, Tamarin, are blood descendants of the same family. Lucinda had no children. Your husband died after Tamarin was born. Is that correct?"

"Yes, he did. Tamarin's daddy was a good man," Mrs. Rowland said. "Half the people on this island got the same last name as ours. But we're the only close family my husband ever had."

Winifred turned to Tamarin. "What that means is, by rights, the old mansion, the ridge, and all of the beach should belong to you and your mother—and whatever other relatives your father has."

Tamarin gasped. "You said mostly good news. What's the bad part?"

It was complicated.

Years ago, the Bahamas had passed a law to promote tourism. The law allowed developers to buy huge portions of land and build hotels, if the land wasn't being used by local people.

"The Quieting Titles Act of 1959," Winifred said. "It's very unfair. Families who have lived here for generations can still be kicked off their property if they don't use their land for a business of some type. Or have what's called a 'clear title.'"

Mrs. Rowland replied, "The only title we got is to this little speck of land. And we're about to lose that 'cause of money I had to borrow."

"Don't worry about the money," Winifred said. She gave

Sabina a private wink, then addressed Tamarin. "You said that, years ago, your father's family owned most of this peninsula. So my lawyer contacted London."

"London, England?" Tamarin asked in disbelief.

"The Bahamas were part of the British Empire back then," Winifred replied. "Most of the land in this area was deeded to one of your great-grandfathers by the king of England. It was during the American Revolution. I think Arthur Katt, the pirate, somehow stole most of it. Either way, the land should belong to you, and other members of the Rowland family."

Tamarin felt a little giddy. Her grin faded when the author warned, "Okay, now here's the bad news."

The company that had loaned Mrs. Rowland money had already filed a claim on all the land surrounding the lagoon. "It's the same company that owns the shark-diving yacht," Winifred said. "They had every legal right to file a claim—or so they thought."

Sabina remembered Red Beard's boast about owning the entire peninsula.

"That's what I came to tell you," Sabina interrupted. "A helicopter and a boat just went past. Right now, the police are probably arresting those men for turtle poaching."

"I'm aware of that." Winifred said this with a sly grin. "But those two fools are just part of the problem. The company they work for builds gambling casinos. They've had their eye on your property for a long, long time. They're based in Las Vegas, Nevada."

Las Vegas, Sabina thought. *I knew it.*

Winifred, as if reading the girl's mind, responded with a private wink. They had spent hours together with Lucinda's diary. Sabina had also shared the truth about the gold coin she had found.

Winifred had seen a similar coin before. It was a rare Spanish doubloon. She guessed it was worth enough to make the Dilly Tree's payment due in seven weeks. More money would be needed to pay off the entire loan, but it was a start.

That was the plan—give the coin to Mrs. Rowland.

Now, sitting at the desk, Winifred recognized the look in Sabina's eyes. Winifred responded with a shake of the head that meant, *We'll tell her about the coin later.*

Winifred continued speaking to Tamarin's mother. "My attorney thinks the church records and your family Bible should be enough to stop the casino developers—for a while, at least. But it would be nice to have more proof that Lucinda Bonny Rowland and Captain Alistar Katt were actually married."

"What other proof is there?" Tamarin asked.

Sabina knew. Last night, as she was crying and clutching the old portrait, Lucinda's eyes had provided the answer. "Her wedding ring," the girl now whispered to her friend, the famous author.

Winifred liked the idea, but said it was nearly impossible. Government permits would be needed to dig up Lucinda's grave. And they weren't even sure the girl was buried there. "Remember Lucinda's gravestone?" Winifred added.

Yes, Sabina remembered. Chiseled into the top of the stone was an angel. An ornate inscription read:

Even in Death, Forever Young

"But the day, month, and year that Lucinda died were never added to the stone," Winifred said patiently. "To the courts, that will suggest she was buried somewhere else."

As the woman spoke, she looked from Tamarin to Mrs. Rowland, and then at her laptop. She noticed today's date. Her face paled despite the rouge on her cheeks. Quickly, she changed the subject.

Later, Winifred took Sabina aside and said, "Josiah was right about Katt Island and its mysteries."

"Preacher Bodden?" the girl asked. "I like him. But what do you mean?"

The famous author replied, "I like him, too. Very much. Let's go for a walk. I think you're the only person who might understand what I'm about to say."

TWENTY-EIGHT

TWO POETS WITH A GIFT

Sabina listened carefully as she and Winifred strolled toward the beach. It was just the two of them, alone in a private world. That's the way it feels when friends, no matter their ages, are together.

The wind gusted. Palm fronds rattled.

In the distance, the helicopter reappeared above the ridge. The patrol boat, blue lights flashing, was already speeding north—perhaps toward the nearest police station.

The turtle poachers were probably inside the boat or the helicopter. Red Beard and Smoky—both from a city named Las Vegas. Sabina had known from the start. It had nothing to do with the design on Red Beard's shirt.

This oddity had been on Winifred's mind for a while.

Her voice softened. "You have a rare gift, my dear," she began. "I'm eighty years old. In all my years, I'm aware of only one other person who had the same unusual gift that you have."

"Was she a famous psychic?" Sabina asked. "I bet she was rich, too."

"No. And yes." The woman sounded wistful. "She was . . . well, let me start over. This girl with the unusual gift was about your age. She wanted to become a poet. Instead, the girl grew up. She chose a career over marriage. An independent life—it wasn't easy for a woman in those days. So she wrote news stories and popular novels to make money. She made so much money that she soon realized that money isn't that important when it comes to a person's dreams. And by then it was too late. The girl didn't entirely waste her gift, but . . . well, that was a long, long time ago."

The sand was soft. Winifred stumbled but caught her balance. Wind had mussed her green cotton-candy hair. She reached and straightened what for the first time Sabina realized was a wig.

An overwhelming sadness flooded the girl. She looked up at the woman and sent a silent message. *You're very sick, Winnie. Why didn't you tell me?*

A nod and a thin, brave smile was the famous author's reply.

"In the library, when I looked at my computer," Winifred continued, "I was shocked when I noticed today's date. You understood why . . . *didn't you*?"

Sabina wanted people to believe that she could read minds. But she couldn't lie to the coolest woman she'd ever met. "I'd be guessing," the girl admitted. She thought for a moment. "Does it have something to do with Lucinda's wedding ring?"

"No. Uh . . . maybe," the woman said. "Do you know what today's date is? I wouldn't have known either if I hadn't checked. On this island, a person loses all track of time."

Sabina replied, "Friday? I'm not sure. I know the moon's supposed to be full tonight. Tamarin mentioned it at breakfast. The Turtle Moon, she said."

"*Exactly.*" Winifred smiled her approval. "Today is Friday, August the thirteenth. On this date, more than one hundred years ago, something very important happened. Remember what we discussed in the library?"

The girl grimaced. Friday the thirteenth was the unluckiest of days. How could she have been so dense? "Of course,"

Sabina said. "Today is Lucinda's wedding anniversary! We should have a party or something. Make a cake, and take flowers to her . . ."

The girl's voice faltered when she remembered something else. In the cemetery, beneath the largest tombstone, a "Man of the Sea" had been buried.

Captain Alistar Katt's name was gone, but the unlucky date of his death had not changed:

August 13, 1910

He had died on their wedding night.

The girl found it difficult to speak.

Winifred, though eighty years old, felt the same romantic sense of loss. "So tragic," she said. "Everyone was against those two young people, but they stayed true to themselves. You have to give them credit for being strong. My guess is, someone used a hammer to remove Alistar Katt's name from the family cemetery. They didn't approve of him marrying Lucinda. Just once in my life, I wish I could have— *had*—met someone so devoted to me that . . ."

The woman couldn't finish the sentence. Her face

squinched as if fighting back tears. An instant later, though, she appeared calm and at peace beneath her makeup.

"Let me tell you something, kiddo," Winifred continued. "There are some real stinkers in this world. But there are also a lot of people with incredible courage. You just don't hear about them much. Those people give me hope." With a sharp smile, the famous author added, "Something to write about, too."

Beyond the beach, the police boat was gone. The helicopter, still visible, resembled a dragonfly over a vast blue lake.

Sabina was indignant. "Turtle poachers murdered Lucinda's husband," she said. "We have to take back what they stole from her."

She was so mad, she didn't notice when the woman's hand stroked her hair.

"We will, my dear," Winifred said. "Strange, huh? You and I are here on the same date, on the same full moon, that it all happened—and more than a hundred years ago." She stopped, the two of them shoulder to shoulder. "Look at me for a moment, would you?"

Sabina turned. Winifred had wise, dark eyes. They

sparkled as if a young girl still lived somewhere deep inside. She placed her hands on Sabina's shoulders.

"I'm going to tell you a secret. I've been after that casino company for a while. A year ago, a mother and her daughter were attacked by sharks because of that yacht. Both died later in the hospital."

Sabina didn't doubt this was true, but asked, "Are you sure? How do you know?"

"Because the mother is my favorite niece." Winifred paused and cleared her throat. "I mean, she *was* my favorite niece. And her daughter was very dear to me. It happened at a resort north of here. They were snorkeling in shallow water—perfectly safe. Or it should have been. They didn't know that the yacht had been in the area chumming up sharks for tourist divers. Your friend, Dr. Ford, confirmed it all when I interviewed him on the phone. That was months ago."

Sabina's expression changed. "Doc has been after those men from the start, hasn't he? Why didn't he tell us?"

Winifred Chase's response was a mild shake of the head. "The point is," she said, "I didn't plan to fall off that yacht. And I certainly didn't expect you kids to save my life. But I don't think it's a coincidence that we met. Or that you found Lucinda's portrait and her diary. What do *you* think, Sabina?"

The girl stared at her bare feet. "Sometimes, at night, Lucinda speaks to me in my sleep. Don't laugh, okay? I don't think she's dead. Not really. That's why there's no date on her grave."

"Won't tell a soul," the woman said. She crossed her heart as if taking an oath. "The portrait you found. Where is it?"

It was in the beach bag Sabina always carried. She took it out. The portrait's frame felt as warm as the cowrie-shell necklace around her neck.

"Let's take it to my cabin," Winifred suggested. "I've got a magnifying glass."

The ring on Lucinda's finger, she explained, had to have been placed there before Alistar Katt drew the portrait of his bride.

"Worth a try, kiddo," Winifred said. "Maybe the artistic sea captain included a detail we've missed."

TWENTY-NINE
LUKE, THE IMAGINARY HERO

Several times, Luke started down the beach toward the cut where the shark-diving yacht was anchored. He wanted to see the government agents in action.

It was so cool. A helicopter and a camouflaged patrol boat had been sent to deal with Red Beard and Smoky. A "sting," Doc had called the operation.

What was the harm in sneaking along the ridge to the cliff? From Captain's Plank, he'd be able to watch the operation go down

A tempting idea. But he couldn't break his promise to the biologist.

In his mind, though, Luke could picture it happening. Soldiers—agents, whatever they were called—dressed in tactical gear, carrying weapons like in a video game. They'd slip aboard the expensive black yacht like Navy SEALs. Hammer on the door a couple of times. Maybe even toss a flash-bang—a harmless explosive—into the cabin.

There would be a *boom*, a lot of smoke. Then Red Beard and Smoky would come stumbling out, hands high, and surrender.

Luke didn't have much of an imagination, according to his teachers. But a bolt of lightning had added a little screen behind his eyes. The screen often portrayed him, an average kid, as a guy with a lot of courage.

The scene continued to play out in his mind.

Red Beard and Smoky, instead of surrendering, would leap into their little rubber dinghy and escape toward shore.

Too bad for them. Instead of freedom, they would see Luke. He would be standing on the beach, unafraid, holding a . . . holding a what?

It had to be a weapon of some type.

That took some thought.

He'd be holding a sharp, three-pronged fish spear, Luke decided. The rubber sling on his wrist was ready to fire if the turtle poachers came any closer.

The look of fear in Red Beard's eyes! The boy grinned, thinking about it.

Red Beard's only option was to turn the rubber boat sharply toward open sea. The government agents, of course, would be busy freeing thousands of baby turtles suffocating in plastic bags. So it was up to the boy to stop the poachers.

No problem. The rubber boat was slow. He would dive into the water, and swim in quiet pursuit until . . .

Luke's imagination hit Pause.

Nope. Diving into the water was a bad idea. That big tiger shark was still hanging around.

He remembered the anchor they had used to save the old lady. The blue nylon rope was real. They had left it in the sand below the cliff.

That could work. Yes . . . he would grab the anchor and hurl it into the dinghy. Red Beard would be clueless until the anchor snagged the little boat's engine, and then—

"Luke!" Maribel hollered. "Hey—did you see the plane?"

She was walking toward him. Her white linen slacks made her legs look longer. A blue tank top added a sheen to her raven-black hair. Maribel looked more like a teenager than a kid who was good at fishing and driving boats.

The boy didn't want to think about that. He cupped his

hands to his eyes. The government chopper was above the ridge. It tilted, nose down, when the patrol boat appeared. Both sped toward them along the beach, then veered away and were soon out of sight.

To Luke, that meant the sting operation was over. He couldn't wait to find out what had happened. Had Red Beard and Smoky been arrested? If so, why wasn't the patrol boat towing their black-hulled yacht to the nearest police station?

When Maribel was closer, she asked again, "Did you see the plane?"

"The chopper, you mean?" Luke said. "Yeah. The patrol boat, too. They're government agents. I think they just busted those guys."

Maribel replied, "Not a helicopter. I'm talking about Dr. Ford's seaplane. I got a glimpse of it from the tree house. When he took off, he stayed so low you probably couldn't see it from here."

"When?"

"Just now."

This was surprising news.

"Are you sure?"

"A small blue-and-white plane," Maribel said. "It turned

north and dropped behind the ridge. Maybe he's going back to Nassau to pick up Hannah and Izaak."

Puzzled, the girl thought for a moment. "I know he and Preacher Bodden were working with the police. But why did Doc come back to help arrest those men?"

"A government agency, not the police," Luke corrected her. "It was a sting operation. Biologists probably help arrest people all the time, because . . ."

Luke couldn't think of a reason. "Maybe it wasn't his plane."

"It was. I'm sure of it." Maribel gave it some thought. "You have to admit, Doc's sort of mysterious sometimes. The way he just disappears. And not even Hannah knows when he's coming back." After another long silence, the girl whispered, "Do you ever wonder if he might be some kind of . . . I don't know, a secret government agent or something?"

Luke gave a snort of laughter. "*Doc?* You kidding? He's smart and all, yeah. But no way. Think about it—he doesn't own a cool car. And all he does is read books and do research and stuff. I doubt if he'd even know how to shoot a gun."

The boy shrugged the silly idea away. He looked toward

the distant ridge. "What matters is, the sting operation's over. It's probably safe now. Think Doc would mind if we walked down the beach and took a look for ourselves?"

It was a long shot. Maribel never broke the rules.

"You know we can't," she said. "Let's go to the lobby. Maybe Mrs. Rowland has heard something. People love to gossip here. Tamarin says news travels fast."

Tamarin's mother was in the kitchen making potato salad. On a cutting board was a large green chili pepper, a bottle of mustard, and a diced onion to be added later.

"Phone's out again," Mrs. Rowland said. "If you want the latest sip-sip, I suggest you two children visit the local grocery store. If those turtle poachers were arrested, that's where folks will know about it."

THIRTY
JELLY COCONUTS
AND GOSSIP

The Dilly Tree Inn had a couple of old bicycles for guests. Luke and Maribel pedaled along a rutted lane to the main road and turned left.

Alfred's Grocery was a simple building of concrete block. In the parking lot, several locals were chatting in the shade—men and women, their ages varied. They waved, and greeted the kids with "Fine, fine, how y'all doin' today?"

Inside, the store was spotless. It was stocked with everything a person might need, from clothing to canned goods. Stalks of bananas lay next to crates of freshly picked limes, oranges, pineapples, hog plums, custard apples, and young, green coconuts.

"A hot day like this, a jelly coconut would be nice," the owner, Alfred Moss, said to Maribel. "I'll cut a couple for you kids, then find out what I can about that charter yacht."

He selected two green coconuts from a cooler and whacked the tops off with a machete.

"You'll need a spoon and some straws," he added. "Have yourselves a seat in the shade where them folks are talking. Don't be shy. They'll for sure know something. My wife, Cindy, saw the helicopter, too."

Luke had eaten dried coconut before. It was nothing like this: a sweet, soft jelly that he and Maribel ate with spoons. First, though, they drank the cold liquid inside. Coconut water—milk, some called it—was delicious.

"Sabina and I break open a young coconut before we wash our hair," Maribel remarked. "Makes your hair so soft and smooth. You ought to try it, next time you shower." With a flick of the hand, the girl tossed back her glossy ponytail as an example.

Luke didn't care if his hair was soft or not. Instead he concentrated on the nearby group of locals. Maribel could hear parts of their conversation, too. Mrs. Rowland had sent them to the right place. The people were talking about what they called "that black-hulled tourist yacht from Miami."

"It's rude to eavesdrop," Maribel reminded the boy. "Let's go over and introduce ourselves."

There was no need. The locals already knew who they were.

"You're Tamarin's friends," a nice lady said. "Been staying at the Dilly Tree. How's Captain Hannah's baby doing? That child come down with a cold, Mrs. Rowland told me. Said Hannah and Dr. Ford are supposed to return from Nassau this afternoon."

A gentleman in a floppy straw hat talked about the best cure for a cold—gargle salt water from the lagoon and drink hot sapodilla tea. Then he added, "Yes, sir, that Dr. Ford sure is a fine man. You kids see the police helicopter fly in this morning? What I heard is, your friend Doc kept a couple of islanders out of that bad business. They say that him and Preacher Bodden been working with the police for a while now to do just that."

It was true about the local sip-sip—gossip.

After that, Luke and Maribel felt right at home. They asked a few questions, but mostly listened.

The man in the straw hat was a fisherman. He'd seen the sting operation, and enjoyed retelling the story. The helicopter had hovered until the patrol boat arrived. Government agents—"soldiers," he called them—had boarded the black-hulled yacht. With them was a police dog.

"It didn't take the soldiers long," the man said. "Over the side, they started dumping bags full of little bitty turtles. Must've been more than a thousand. Oh man, did those baby turtles swim away fast. Another soldier there, she had a camera. Got it all on video, I expect."

The best part came next. The "soldiers" had arrested two people.

"One fella had a thick red beard," the man in the straw hat said. "Other fella, sort of tall. Got mad when the soldiers wouldn't let him smoke a cigarette. That's probably why they put handcuffs on him before they carted those two off."

"They didn't handcuff them both?" someone asked.

"Probably did later," the man said, "on the way back to Nassau. No need at the time. The bearded fella, he acted very polite and respectful."

The nice lady mentioned her nephew. "A week ago, I told that boy to stay away from those fellas. What I heard is, they were offering money to the young folks here to rob turtle nests. I told him, 'Don't be a fool. A few dollars aren't worth jail in Nassau.' Thank heavens none of our local people got involved."

The man in the straw hat didn't respond. Instead he cleared his throat in a way that seemed to warn, *No more talking about that.*

The nice lady, suddenly quiet, turned away.

There was an uncomfortable silence before the man spoke again.

"When you see your friend Dr. Ford," he said to Maribel and Luke, "you mind giving him a message?"

Maribel realized what the problem was. The local people couldn't talk freely with them around. "Of course," she said. "We have to get back to the Dilly Tree for dinner soon, anyway."

The man in the straw hat was pleased that she understood. "Tell him that a friend of Preacher Bodden says hello. We sure appreciate what Doc has done for the folks on this island."

His eyes moved to Luke. "You too, young fella."

Biking home to the Dilly Tree, Maribel asked, "Why do you think he thanked you?"

"No idea," the boy said. It was a lie. Sort of. Luke had figured out the connection between the Boiling Blue Hole and Whale Mouth Cave. There was another surprising detail that he had confided only to the biologist. And Doc had confirmed that Luke's suspicions were correct.

"News sure travels fast here," Maribel said. "Tamarin was right. I can't wait to tell her and Sabina what we just heard."

Luke suspected that Tamarin already knew.

He was more concerned about something else. It was possible that Red Beard had not been handcuffed. It was unlikely, but . . . what if the man hadn't been arrested?

Worse, what if Red Beard had escaped?

THIRTY-ONE
SABINA AND THE BEAUTIFUL GHOST

After sunset on the thirteenth of August, an orange moon boiled up through the trees in the lagoon. By bedtime, the moon was huge, bright as a midnight sun. Outside Sabina's window, waxen coconut palms glowed like candles. A storm wind echoed with distant lightning.

The girl tossed and turned but couldn't sleep. She gave up, found a flashlight, and pulled the covers over her head.

On the other side of the room, Maribel's soft breathing remained undisturbed.

Sabina often read beneath the covers. It was quiet, private, like being inside a tent. Instead of a book, she opened the wooden box she'd found. It contained the diary of the teenager whose gravestone had been left un-finished.

More than one hundred years ago, on this same unlucky night, while an orange moon blazed, something terrible had happened. Alistar Katt, the artistic sea captain, had been murdered.

How? And what had become of Lucinda?

Sabina leafed through a few brittle pages, then returned the diary to the box. There was more to be learned from the beautiful teenager's portrait. It was beneath her pillow with the gold coin.

Sabina tilted the flashlight to see better. The brass frame felt warmer than the night air. Haunting dark eyes looked back and observed Sabina's every move.

The eyes came alive. Lucinda's hands, folded beneath her chin, demanded attention. On the fourth finger of her left hand was the ring, drawn by Alistair.

Thanks to Winifred's magnifying glass, details were still fresh in Sabina's mind. On the ring, the face of an angel had been etched into gold. On her head was a crown. In place of wings, the angel wore a musical instrument called a harp.

"It's a signet ring," Winifred had explained. "For hundreds of years, people used melted wax to seal letters and documents. A signet ring was pressed into the wax as a signature. The family crest, it was called. Or a coat of arms."

The engraving on Lucinda's ring had a special meaning.

On their visits to the mansion, Winifred had taken a lot of photographs. One was a close-up of the old brass bell found near the gate. The bell had the same engraving.

An angel who wore harp strings for wings, and a gold crown.

"The symbol was Captain Katt's family signature—or crest," the author had explained. "Legally, that's important. But the portrait doesn't prove the ring was actually given to Lucinda on her wedding day. Lawyers might say the ring never existed. That the artist made it up."

Winifred had seen the strange symbol before. She couldn't remember where, exactly, but had promised to do more research.

Sabina, huddled beneath the covers with a flashlight, knew the ring was real. She focused on the teenage girl's face, and tried to communicate silently.

Speak to me, she pleaded. *Where are you? You can trust me, Lucinda. I promise.*

Over and over, she voiced those words in her mind.

Speak to me . . . Please trust me.

A grumble of thunder swirled through the trees. The cabin floor, cradled by tree limbs, shifted like the deck of a boat.

Sabina clutched her cowrie necklace and listened to the wind. The wind was how the dead communicated.

There was no response from Lucinda.

The girl settled back, her head on the pillow. Into her mind floated the image of Lucinda's gravestone. For a century, that simple white stone had sat alone, unfinished, protected by a giant tree.

Sabina began to recite the inscription on the stone. The words matched her slow breathing.

Even in Death . . . Forever Young . . .
Even in Death . . . Forever Young . . .

Soon the girl was asleep—or thought she was asleep—until she heard a soft tapping at the cabin door.

Sabina threw the covers back, convinced it was her imagination. A distant flash of lightning, though, suggested it might be Luke. The boy was scared of storms. So she dressed in a hurry and, for some reason, carried the wooden box to the door.

"Mother of stars," she whispered in Spanish when the door was open.

Outside, on the tree-house platform, stood a beautiful teenage girl. She wore a white nightgown. The gown shimmered like silk in the moonlight. A whiff of coconut glossed the girl's wind-tangled hair.

Sabina glanced back at Maribel. How could her sister still be asleep?

In a voice that was soft, but real, the teenage girl spoke. "My mahogany box. Good," she said. "I wanted you to find my diary before someone else did. The Spanish coin, too. Hurry—it'll be midnight soon."

The beautiful girl held out a hand. A gold ring sparkled on her finger.

Sabina hesitated. She looked into the most haunting dark eyes she'd ever seen, then grasped the teenager's hand. The girl's skin felt warm and young and alive.

"Am I dreaming?" Sabina asked.

"Does it matter?" replied Lucinda Bonny Rowland. "You said I can trust you. We have to run—or we'll be too late."

THIRTY-TWO
SABINA SLEEPWALKS, RED BEARD ESCAPES

The pounding Luke heard slipped into his dreams. He was back in Ohio, in the barn, pounding a nail with a hammer. The hammer missed and whacked his thumb.

Typical.

Somehow this caused him to fall out of the hayloft.

"Ouch!" he said when he hit the floor.

The boy sat up. He'd fallen out of bed, not a hayloft. And someone was pounding at his cabin door.

"Hold your horses, I'm coming," he hollered.

Rather than risk embarrassment, he dressed and checked his face for dried toothpaste before seeing who was there.

It was Maribel. "My sister's gone," she said in a panic. "We have to find her."

Above a canopy of palms, lightning flickered. Far out to sea, green clouds glowed for an instant. They showed a distant helicopter zooming away from bad weather.

Was it the same helicopter they'd seen earlier? And why was it flying on a stormy night like this?

Immediately, Luke thought of Red Beard. The man hadn't been handcuffed.

"Where'd Sabina go?" the boy asked.

"I don't know," Maribel said. "She left our cabin door open. That's what woke me up. By the time I got outside, I got a glimpse of her near the beach. I think she's walking in her sleep again."

Luke wasn't eager to leave the tree house—not with a storm coming. And the helicopter wasn't proof that Red Beard had actually escaped.

"Running toward the beach, or walking?" he asked. "Either way, Sabina will wake up when she hits the water."

He yawned and checked his watch—a rubber G-Shock he'd bought with his own money.

"For cripes' sakes," he added, "it's a quarter after eleven. It'll be midnight before we get back to bed."

Good boat captains never lose their temper. Maribel came close. "We're a team," she reminded the boy. "I'm not going to order you to help—but I could. Think about all the times you got lost. Sabina and I pretended not to know, but we did. And we always came looking for you."

Many times in Luke's life, he'd been scolded for doing one dumb thing or another. But never by Doc or Hannah— or Maribel.

Of the three, suddenly, Maribel was the last person in the world he wanted to disappoint.

Over the ocean, silent thunder stamped the sky with a lightning bolt. Darkness cast shadows beneath a rust-red moon.

In the moonlight, Maribel wore a raincoat over a white, knee-length nightshirt, as if she'd just gotten out of bed. "Put some clothes on," Luke said. "I'll get my backpack and another flashlight."

"I already have a flashlight," Maribel insisted. "There's no time. There might be turtle poachers out tonight."

Luke shouldered his backpack anyway, and followed the girl down the bamboo steps, through palm trees.

On the beach, they stopped. "Which way did Sabina go?" he asked.

"I have no idea." Maribel sounded panicky again. "It's been at least five minutes since I saw her. Maybe ten." From the pocket of her raincoat, she removed a flashlight.

"Don't use that," Luke said. "I won't be able to see anything. Give me a second."

He did a slow, searching turn. The helicopter was gone. A mile of white sand sparkled beneath the moon. Far, far, in the distance, a skipping shadow resembled a young girl having fun.

"There she is," Luke said. "It's like she's playing a game. Maybe holding someone's hand."

"Where?" Maribel asked. "Is she with Tamarin? I haven't seen her since dinner."

It was true. The last two nights, Tamarin had disappeared after sunset.

The boy couldn't be sure who the second person was. One girlish shadow sometimes appeared to separate and become two people.

Maribel strained to see, then gave up. "How far?"

"Half a mile," Luke guessed. "She's almost to the ridge where we found the banana hole. We'll have to run to catch her."

They did.

Maribel sprinted like a deer. The boy struggled to keep up.

They charged past the path to the banana hole, and kept going. Somehow, Sabina's playful shadow remained several hundred yards ahead.

Finally, Luke had to stop. He was so winded, he put his hands on his knees to speak. "She's . . . she's headed for where the shark-diving yacht's anchored. Why would she go there?"

Ahead, the beach curved sharply. High above was the black outline of a cliff.

Captain's Plank, Maribel realized. "Luke, we have to keep going. Do you still see her?"

"Yeah," he said. "She's almost to the spot where we saved Winifred. She can't go much farther without waking up—or falling into the water."

The boy took time to get his bearings. To the left was a familiar wall of vines. He listened. A waterfall spilling onto rocks blended with the sound of a storm coming from offshore.

The cave, he thought. *Whale Mouth Cave.*

In the sand, a thousand feathered turtle tracks confirmed he was right. The tracks had been dusted by a moon-bright wind.

Larger, deeper tracks caught his attention. They were the heavy footprints of an adult—a man, probably. The tracks angled away from the beach toward the cave.

"Maybe she can hear me if I holler," Maribel said. She cupped her hands and began to call Sabina's name.

Before Luke could stop her, a shadow emerged from the trees. It was a man, large and muscular. He came limping toward them, carrying a long-bladed knife in one hand. A machete. "I'm hurt bad," he called. "I stepped on something—some kind of poison fish. You kids better help me, or you'll be sorry."

It was Red Beard.

Luke and Maribel stood motionless. They would have run if they hadn't recognized a smaller person behind the man.

It was Tamarin.

"There won't be any trouble," Red Beard said, "if you do exactly what I tell you. Got that?"

"Depends on what it is," Maribel replied stubbornly.

"None of your sass talk!" the man snapped. He limped closer. "You kids are going to swim out to my yacht. There's a little boat tied off the back. A red dinghy. I want you to start the motor and bring it back to the beach."

"Swim?" Maribel said.

"You heard me. It's not that far."

This was nuts, and Luke knew it. "No way, mister. There are too many sharks—all because of you."

A thread of lightning showed the man's haggard face. "Don't argue! Do what I say, and your little friend here won't go to jail. Does that sound so hard?"

"Jail?" Maribel looked to Tamarin.

In the bright moonlight, the local girl refused to make eye contact.

Luke had already guessed why.

"Sorry," Tamarin said softly. "If you don't help him, he'll tell the police I've been selling baby turtles. I'm a thief, and I don't blame you if you never speak to me again."

THIRTY-THREE
MOON-WRECKERS OR A DREAM?

Sabina felt like she could fly when she took Lucinda's hand. The teenage girl's gown billowed with moonlight as they ran down the beach to the ridge.

There was no need to speak because their hands were joined. Their thoughts flowed in silence.

At the path to the banana hole, Sabina tried to slow. Thunder grumbled. The first fat drops of rain began to fall. Tucked under her arm was the black wooden box.

Are we going to the mansion? Sabina wondered.

Lucinda's face was ghostly pale. She looked toward the ridge. "That's where the asylum was. I hated it there. They claimed I was crazy. The cemetery, yes—but only if we're in time to help my husband."

She meant Alistar Katt, the artistic sea captain.

Sabina thought, *But he's already dead. I saw his gravestone.*

Lucinda's voice had the low tones of a flute. "He didn't die; he was murdered. For years, on this night, my wedding night, I've prayed for someone like you to come. Finally, you're here. I trust you, Sabina. My secret will stay safe. You'll know what to do when we get there."

Get where? Sabina thought. *How will I know?*

Rather than answer, the pretty teenager's face tilted skyward. "Feel the rain? You poor dear, you'll be soaked. There was a storm that night, too. And a full moon—the full moon's always highest at midnight. Did you know that?"

The full moon is always highest at midnight, Sabina repeated in her head.

"Hurry," Lucinda whispered. "This will be my last chance to change what happened. We don't have much time."

They ran toward the inlet where the shark-diving yacht had been anchored. High above was the black outline of a cliff—Captain's Plank. Below, silver water flowed from open sea.

The yacht was gone. Instead an old sailing ship had rammed itself into the shallows. Someone had hung lanterns on a pole as if the sandbar were a deep channel. The ship's captain had been tricked into wrecking his own boat.

It was the same sandbar where the kids had saved Winifred's life.

The sailing ship appeared to be empty. "Where'd the crew go?" Sabina wondered.

"To get revenge," Lucinda answered. "They're up there now—turtle poachers and thieves. Alistar is the one who tricked them into running aground. He hung those lanterns, then took a hundred gold coins as a wedding present to me after their boat wrecked. But they caught him."

"Your husband, Captain Katt?" Sabina wondered.

"Yes. My dear, dear Alistar. Tonight's our wedding night. Can you see him?"

Clouds blackened the moon. Atop the cliff, flames sparked in the wind. Men with torches had gathered at the edge of the cliff.

It was raining harder now. Impossible to look up and see details.

Sabina used the wooden box as a shield. When she did,

a terrible scene floated into her mind. Sailors, roughly dressed, had captured a tall, slim man. Rain soaked his braided hair. A flash of lightning showed the face of Alistar Katt. It was a lean face with fierce eyes. His hands were bound behind him.

One of the sailors had a pistol. They were forcing Captain Katt toward the edge of the cliff.

"We have to stop them," Sabina yelled. They were at the path that led uphill.

Lucinda's woodwind voice answered, "You've come as far as you can go."

"No, I hate turtle poachers. I want to help!"

"You will—when you understand," the musical voice responded. "That night, I should have fought for the one I love. But I was a coward. Years later, maybe I did go crazy. I came here alone and I . . . I did what no person has the right to do."

Sabina wiped the water from her eyes. Another horrible scene flashed into her mind. Lucinda, no longer young, was alone on the cliff, walking toward the edge.

"I wanted to join Alistar," said the beautiful girl from the portrait. "It was so easy . . . and so *wrong*. I destroyed our hope of finding peace. But it's not too late—thanks to you. My mahogany box, Sabina. Give me the box. It was a wedding present, too."

Sabina turned and did it. Lucinda's face was a mist of rain and shadows. Their hands joined. For an instant, their fingers shared a comforting warmth.

Lucinda pulled away, then started up the path to the cliff. After a few steps, she appeared to sag in the blinding rain, and nearly dropped the box.

Sabina extended her arms to help. There was a buzzing sound. An explosion of thunder followed. A nearby palm tree blazed in a shower of sparks.

When she looked again, the girl from the portrait was nearly to the cliff. "Wait for me!" Sabina hollered, and charged up the hill.

Wind echoed with what sounded like gunshots. Clouds veiled a moon that was high in the midnight sky.

The path narrowed. When Sabina reached the top, she wondered if she'd made a wrong turn. Rain had slowed to a drizzle. A fleet of orange clouds parted. The moon reappeared.

There were no sailors with torches.

The beautiful teenage girl and the artistic sea captain were gone.

Confused, Sabina wandered toward the edge of the cliff, hollering Lucinda's name.

Finally, there was a terrified response from far below. "Wake up! Sabina, wake up!"

It was Maribel's voice, screaming at her.

"Stop . . . stop! Wake up. It's me!"

Sabina blinked her eyes clear and looked down. Everything had changed. The shark-diving yacht was anchored where it was supposed to be. Lanterns no longer hung from a post on the sandbar. The old sailing ship had vanished.

Had it all been a dream?

On the beach below, Luke switched on a flashlight. The beam was so bright, Sabina had to cover her eyes and turn away.

"Stupid farm boy," she muttered in Spanish, then said, "Ouch." She had kicked something with her shoe.

At her feet, in the moonlight, was the wooden box.

Sabina knelt and opened it.

The diary was gone.

Across the distance, Maribel hollered, "Answer me, Sabina! You're sleepwalking. We need your help!"

The girl stood taller, glared, and yelled, "I'm wide

awake—don't rush me." She was still confused and a little angry. If she'd been dreaming, where was the diary?

Sabina tucked the box under her arm. She started downhill, arguing with herself.

It wasn't a dream . . . Or was it a dream? Maybe she had left the diary on her bed.

On the path, rocks glowed with gray light. It was brighter there. To make sure the box really was empty, she reached to open the lid—and, for the first time, understood.

"Mother of stars," Sabina whispered.

She raised her right hand toward the moon. On her index finger was Lucinda's gold ring. The ghost of the teenager had transferred the ring to Sabina's finger when they had clasped hands.

A windy, flute-like voice reminded Sabina, *Keep my secret safe. You'll know what to do when you get there.*

THIRTY-FOUR
CAPTURED BY RED BEARD

Luke had never seen a person in as much pain as Red Beard. The man bullied them down the beach to where his yacht was anchored, then collapsed in the sand.

Cuss words were followed by grunting sounds. He complained of dizziness and a headache.

That's when Maribel saw Sabina on the cliff and started yelling.

"Be quiet!" Red Beard ordered the older sister. "My head's killing me as it is. Let her jump, for all I care. I don't want that little witch around me."

Maribel refused to obey. That made him madder. He used the machete as a cane and tried to get to his feet, but fell.

There was more swearing, more threats. "You kids are getting on my nerves. All you've got to do is swim to my dinghy and bring it back here. Do that, you'll never see me again. Which one of you is the fastest swimmer?"

Luke switched on a flashlight. When he was sure Sabina was on the path downhill, he shined the light on Red Beard. "Mister, you either stepped on a stingray or a lionfish. Either way, you need to get to a hospital. Let me take a look at your foot. I've got a first-aid kit in my bag."

"A lionfish?" the man groaned. "You don't know what you're talking about."

The flashlight showed Red Beard's left tennis shoe. Colorful stingers had pierced the shoe and gone through his foot. "Yep, a lionfish." Luke nodded. "Seriously, you could die if you don't get to a hospital."

"Bull!" the man said. "You're making that up. Trying to scare me. A bag of ice and a beer, that's all I need."

"Ice would make it worse," the boy responded. "Soaking your foot in hot water might take the pain away. Those stingers have to be removed or you could pass out. Maybe even stop breathing." He placed his backpack on the ground and opened it. "I've got some stuff in here that might help."

Tamarin had lagged behind. "Should I run and call a doctor?"

"No!" The man managed to get to his feet. He motioned with the machete. "You're staying right here with me. If the cops come, they'll arrest you, too. Understand?"

The long-bladed knife swung toward Luke, then Maribel. "I'm gonna ask you kids one more time. Who's the fastest swimmer?"

Maribel and Luke spoke at the same time, saying, "I am."

Red Beard lowered the machete. "Noble, huh? Little brats," he said. "Fine. Then you're both going. Hurry up. Get in the water now."

Sabina was on the beach, walking toward them. Rain had slowed, but electricity still flickered in the sky. Maribel replied, "Not until I make sure my sister's all right."

Red Beard watched the girls hug, and whisper back and forth in Spanish. He didn't like that. "Time's up. Get moving!" he said.

Luke had already taken off his boots. Next came his T-shirt. "Mister, what kind of engine does your dinghy have? I'm worried it won't start, and we'll have to swim back. There are some big sharks around here, and you know it."

The man from Las Vegas found that funny. "That's

right, I'm not stupid. Why do you think I'm making you kids get in the water?" He managed a wincing smile.

Luke walked away. In the distance, the yacht's black hull glistened. The vessel was longer than three school buses and tall as a house. The mouth of the inlet was narrow. In the milky light, the water's surface resembled a frozen lake. To most people, the sandbar was invisible.

He waited for Maribel to join him at the water's edge.

"We can't let that guy get away," he whispered. "He doesn't know anything about boats. Hopefully, he'll hit the sandbar when he tries to leave."

"We have to play along—for now," Maribel responded.

The boy glanced at her, then looked away. Maribel was taking off her raincoat.

"What do you mean, 'play along'?"

"We'd be crazy to swim because of the sharks. So I told Sabina to wait until we wade into the shallows, then grab Tamarin and run. The guy will be watching us, not them. Then we'll run, too. With his bad foot, he won't be able to catch us."

Maribel placed her rain jacket on the beach, saying, "Let's go."

Luke followed her into the water. The current was

strong. It dug the sand from beneath their feet. He started to ask about Tamarin's fear of the police, but didn't get the words out.

"I told you kids, no tricks!" roared Red Beard. The man was stumbling toward them, machete raised. Already too close for them to high-step out of the water and escape.

Luke tried anyway. He splashed toward shore, but lost his footing. Immediately, the current swept him into deep water.

Maribel hollered, "Run, Sabina, run!"

And plunged in after Luke.

THIRTY-FIVE
RED BEARD'S PROMISE

Sabina was already sprinting toward the hotel when her sister yelled, "Run!"

The girl stopped. She released Tamarin's hand and looked back. The bad man had Maribel and Luke trapped at the edge of the sandbar.

Sabina watched Luke and her sister disappear into the water. Red Beard started to follow, then staggered and collapsed in the bright moonlight.

"Keep going," she told Tamarin. "You're faster than me. Tell your mother to call for help, then wake up Winifred. She'll know what to do."

The local girl saw what had happened. "I can't leave

your sister. She's my friend. That coconut-head boy, too. Are there really sharks out there?"

Sabina sensed there was another concern. "Don't worry. When Doc and Hannah get back from Nassau, they won't let the police arrest you. Winifred will protect you, too. I promise."

"What about him?" Tamarin insisted, meaning Red Beard. He lay groaning in the sand. "It's not just me I'm worried about. There are kids on this island who needed money as bad as me. Selling baby turtles is wrong, I know it. But we're like family on this island. I can't let them get in trouble because I ran away."

Tamarin had made up her mind. They jogged back to the inlet. Red Beard saw them. He sat up, holding his stomach as if he was about to vomit.

"Get away from me, you little witch," he said when he recognized Sabina. "I don't know how, but I think you got me into this mess. You and your magic spells." He fumbled for the machete. "Stay back, or I'll hit you. I mean it!"

Tamarin stopped in her tracks. Sabina kept going. She was scared enough to be mad. She believed Lucinda's wooden box and ring would provide protection. Her cowrie-shell necklace was powerful, too.

"Try it," the girl shouted, "and I'll put another hex on you. You stepped on a lionfish. If we don't help, you could die."

A thunderous bolt of lightning stopped her a few yards from the man. She could see that he was in agony.

"Dying's better than having to listen to a stupid little girl," Red Beard snarled. He tried to threaten her with the machete again but fell back in the sand. "Help me how?" he mumbled. "My foot . . . it's killing me. Feels like I'm burning up."

Sabina's anger faded. It was hard to stay mad at a person who was suffering. She placed the wooden box on the ground and removed her necklace. The tiny seashells were cool to the touch.

"Hold these," she said.

Red Beard looked up. His face was feverish. So feverish that he saw a witch with braids, not a little girl, standing over him. The big white moon above the witch formed a halo. "Leave me alone. I mean it, stay back!" he groaned. "Your eyes . . . they're like the eyes of a black cat."

Thunder rumbled. The storm's last cold raindrops blew toward them from the sea.

"I love cats," Sabina replied. She forced the beads into

the man's hands. His skin was rough and hot, slick with sweat. "Close your eyes," she ordered. "Take deep breaths. The pain's already going away, isn't it?"

Sabina mumbled a magic spell she had learned in Cuba from the women in white. She hoped it would work. The girl was more concerned about Maribel and Luke. For a few seconds, their heads had been visible in the current streaming toward the yacht. Now they were gone.

It took a while. Red Beard licked his lips. His chest heaved. In a whisper, he muttered the foulest sort of words. He pulled the necklace to his chest. A minute passed, and his breathing began to slow. Surprised, the man's eyes blinked open. "It's working. The pain . . . seems to be going away. How'd you do that?"

Tamarin had approached quietly. She knelt, grabbed the machete from the ground, then jumped back a safe distance.

Red Beard saw her. He gave a howling yelp when he tried to sit.

"We won't stop you from escaping," Sabina said. "But you've got to promise something, or the pain will come back."

The man stared. His expression changed. "This is crazy. You really are a witch."

Sabina's courage had faded with her anger. She couldn't let Red Beard see that she was scared. "We'll help you get into your boat. If the police catch you, though, you have to swear not to tell them about Tamarin."

"Or any of my friends," Tamarin added. Her voice was shaking. She didn't raise the machete, but held it tightly in her hand.

"You've got to swear," Sabina insisted. "If you lie to me, no matter where you are, the pain will come back. Understand? It'll never go away."

Red Beard made a blowing sound through his lips. "Crazy little brats," he muttered.

Sabina found Luke's backpack. When she opened the first-aid kit, though, the man finally said, "Okay. I swear."

THIRTY-SIX
SWIMMING WITH A TIGER SHARK

The sudden blast of lightning took Luke's mind off the shark fin he'd seen cruising toward them.

Maribel hadn't noticed the dark swirl ahead. They had joined hands and let the incoming tide push them toward the yacht. It was better to drift with their legs dangling. Swimming was too risky. Splashing might attract attention.

This was Maribel's idea.

"We're okay," she said after the lightning strike. Luke had yanked his hand away. "We're almost there."

Not close enough, the boy thought.

The fin had surfaced in a tunnel of moonlight. The

yacht was twenty yards beyond. To get to the yacht, they'd have to swim past the shark—a big one.

The tiger shark, Luke decided. Its fin had thrown a massive shadow as it submerged.

"To heck with Red Beard," he whispered to Maribel. "The girls ran away. They're safe by now. You said so yourself. I think we should get the heck out of the water."

In the swift current, they had to use their hands like rudders. Sort of like floating down a river in an inner tube, which he'd done back in Ohio. But there were no inner tubes to save them if something grabbed their legs from below.

"It's too late for that," Maribel said. "Besides, Tamarin might be arrested. What else can we do?"

To their left, the rocky shoreline wasn't far away. High above was the cliff. Lightning had zapped a tree there. Flames showered down like lava from a volcano.

Luke kept his voice low. "We need to get to shore as fast as we can." He nodded toward the rocks. "From there we can follow the ridge back to the hotel. We'll worry about the police later."

Maribel sensed his sudden fear. She steered her body close enough to bump shoulders. "What's wrong? You saw something, didn't you? Or is it because of the lightning?"

Luke said again, "We've got to get out of the water *now*."

"The tiger shark?" Maribel whispered.

The boy started to lie, but couldn't. "Yeah, something big near the yacht. For all I know, it's coming toward us right now."

The girl's head swung toward the black-hulled yacht. Nothing there but glittering moonlight and the silhouette of antennas.

They both had to fight the same temptation—to swim as fast as they could to the beach. But they knew too much about sharks to panic.

Maribel, after a deep breath, took charge. "Okay, we'll head for shore. But stay calm, go slow. Pull your knees up to your chest. Like we're a couple of beach balls."

Side by side, the kids turned. They began to glide away from the yacht toward land. No splashing, no kicking. Their hands used the current to steer silently. Soon the earthy scent of wet vines blended with the odor of lightning and open sea.

"Think we're close enough to touch bottom?" Luke asked.

Maribel extended her legs. Her toes found nothing but

deep water and darkness. Slowly, she curled her knees back to her chest. "Not yet," she replied.

Overhead, a cloud sailed across the moon. Thunder cast a slow, snaking shadow on the water's surface. Luke noticed it first. The shadow glided past them, then turned in the shallows near shore.

"Oh, crapola," he whispered. "Do you see it?"

A triangle of gray, three feet high, pivoted toward them. A giant scythe-like tail stirred the water. The fin submerged.

The tiger shark knew Luke and Maribel were there.

"Swim for the boat," Maribel yelled, because there was nothing else they could do.

She put her head down and swam just as hard as she could. Because of her sodden nightshirt, Luke got there first. The little rubber dinghy was tied to the stern of the yacht. He grabbed the line and climbed to safety.

Maribel arrived a moment later. "Take my hand!" he hollered to the girl.

Clouds had parted. The tiger shark's fin sliced the moonlight only a few yards behind Maribel's legs. Maribel felt something bump her left hip. Fear, with the help of Luke's hand, vaulted her into the little boat.

They collapsed together on the deck, breathing heavily.

Then, for no reason, they began to laugh. That's how scared they were. Luke, who seldom spoke, couldn't get the words out fast enough. Same with Maribel.

"Was that crazy or what?"

"Are you kidding? Insane. I can't wait to tell Sabina and Tamarin about this."

Luke got to his feet and began to search the water. "No one will believe us. Tiger shark, dude. I'd bet on it. Did you know it was right behind you?"

"My God, really?" Maribel laughed. "That was freaky. I felt something bang into my leg. Like sandpaper, as big as a car."

The girl stood. She inspected her left thigh. "See . . . right there. That's where it scraped me. Took some of the skin off. Luke—it could have bitten me in half!"

She continued talking about what had just happened. The boy stared. Suddenly silent, he knelt to inspect the dinghy's little outboard motor.

"What's wrong?" Maribel asked. She feared the shark had returned.

"We can't help that guy escape. I'm trying to think of a way to stop him."

As captain of Sharks Incorporated, Maribel knew more

about boats than most adults. This included Red Beard. "What do you have in mind?"

Luke said, "First, let's make sure we can get this thing started."

On the deck of the dinghy was a plastic gas tank. The tank was connected to the engine by a rubber hose. He squeezed the primer bulb and yanked the starter cord.

The little engine sputtered and coughed and clattered to life.

Maribel made the long step from the dinghy up onto the yacht's swim platform. There was a ladder there. "One way to stop him," she said, "is to find the yacht's radio and call for help. I'll search the cabin while you figure something out."

"I already have," Luke said. "While you're up there, find a knife. Something sharp."

"A weapon?" Maribel shook her head in disapproval. "You've got to be kidding. We can't do that."

"That's not what I mean," the boy said. "Halfway back to the beach, I'll disconnect the fuel tank. Or cut the hose. Maybe both. He won't know until the carburetor gets sucked dry. This engine will run for a few minutes at least."

"You're setting a trap for Red Beard." Maribel was grinning. "That's so smart—and brave!"

Luke felt his face flush. "A *sting*, Doc calls it. If the guy tries to escape, he won't get far without fuel."

Maribel disappeared up the ladder, saying, "You come up with the best ideas sometimes. I won't be long."

THIRTY-SEVEN
MAYDAY, MAYDAY!

The tiger shark hadn't given up. Its tail churned the water behind the dinghy while Luke waited for Maribel to return. In the moonlight, the fin surfaced again beneath the cliff.

Doc would want to hear about the shark's behavior. Long after the tourist divers were gone, sharks still associated people with food. It explained the recent attacks on snorkelers in the clear, shallow water of the Bahamas.

Well . . . that was Luke's opinion, he had to admit. More proof was needed. But not now. He and Maribel had had enough close calls for one night.

The boy's confidence began to improve. Storm clouds slid past with the last of the rain. Thunder rumbled, but no more nearby lightning strikes. All they had to do now was get back to the beach. Red Beard would take the dinghy and try to escape—until he ran out of gas.

Hopefully.

Luke experimented with the little boat's motor by stopping and restarting it. It was a four-horsepower Mercury with a simple tiller arm for steering. On the farm, he had kept their tractor and lawn mower running. His grades hadn't been great, but he knew about spark plugs and leaky fuel lines.

A four-horse Mercury would continue to run for a while if the gas tank was disconnected. Or the fuel hose was cut. But for how long, the boy wasn't sure. He was messing with the hose when Maribel reappeared. She hadn't been gone long.

"Luke," she hissed from above him. "We've got to get back to the beach right away." She came down the ladder in a rush.

The panic in her voice didn't allow questions. The boy waited until she was aboard the dinghy to ask, "Why? What's wrong?"

The cabin of the yacht had provided a better view of the beach, Maribel explained. Her sister and Tamarin had not run away as planned.

Maribel had seen them with Red Beard. The man was on his feet again.

"Does he still have the machete?"

"Probably. He's too far away to be sure. Let's go!"

They untied the dinghy and pushed away from the yacht. Luke steered because he already knew how to work the motor. Maribel knew that sound carried over water, so she scooted closer and spoke into Luke's ear.

"We have to pretend we want Red Beard to escape. You're not a very good liar, so try not to say too much."

The boy couldn't argue with that.

"Just play innocent. Don't argue with him. Oh—and pretend like you're scared."

"That won't be hard," Luke replied.

"Good. We'll give him the dinghy, then run away the first chance we get. I wanted to shut off the yacht's battery switches, but I didn't have time. So if he makes it aboard the yacht, he'll be able to start the engines. I must've panicked. Sorry."

"What about a knife?" Luke asked.

"I was looking for one in the main cabin. That's when I saw him grab Sabina and I just sort of lost it."

"He *grabbed* her?" Luke twisted the throttle, but the motor wouldn't go any faster. "What a dipstick."

"Or maybe he leaned on her to keep from falling. Hope so, anyway. I couldn't believe the girls were still there. I found the radio and called for help, then took off."

"You called Mayday?"

On a VHF marine radio, Mayday meant "emergency": A boater needed help right away. VHF was a "very high frequency" radio used by travelers around the world, including the Coast Guard. The signal could be heard on boats and planes many miles away—if someone was listening.

Maribel was getting emotional. "I don't know if anyone answered me or not. I was too scared to stick around and wait. If that man hurts my sister or Tamarin, I'll—I'll—"

"There he is," Luke interrupted.

The beach was fifty yards away. Red Beard and the girls were three misty silhouettes. They were moving toward the sound of the dinghy's outboard motor.

Luke also noticed a flashing light far out to sea. "What's that?"

Maribel thought he'd seen something on the beach. She squinted at the shadows of her sister and Tamarin. "Don't know. They were a lot easier to see from the yacht. It's so much higher."

"Not them. Out there."

The boy pointed to the ocean, then blinked several times. Inside his head, a circle of blue projected an image. Speeding toward them was a helicopter. Maybe the same chopper he'd seen earlier.

"They heard you," he said softly.

"Who?"

"The police, maybe. Someone heard your Mayday call," Luke said. "Or Doc's friends."

The girl still didn't understand.

"Government agents," Luke explained.

He touched a finger to his lips, meaning, *Quiet*. At the last minute, he yanked the fuel hose free of the little outboard motor. To make sure the hose couldn't be used, he tied it in a knot.

They didn't say another word until the dinghy banged onto the beach.

THIRTY-EIGHT
STINGERS!

Red Beard was in the water waiting when Luke and Maribel arrived in the dinghy. The man limped when he walked, but didn't appear to be in as much pain.

"Took you brats long enough," he growled. He blinded them with a flashlight and splashed closer. "Get out, hurry. Hey, you, kid!" He meant Luke. "Don't shut off that engine."

Luke had no intention of shutting off the engine. He wanted to burn all the fuel that was left inside the carburetor. The man rolled himself into the little boat and sat at the tiller after the boy had jumped out.

Sabina appeared. She crossed the beach, yelling, "Hey—I want my necklace back."

Maribel had to stop her when Red Beard held up the cowrie shells like a trophy.

"Tough luck, little girl." He grinned. "From now on, I don't go anywhere without your magic necklace." On his wrist, good-luck horseshoes tinkled.

"You'll be sorry," Sabina warned. She was trying to battle her way free. "I told you what will happen if you break your promise."

The man found that funny. "My promise? *Right.* We'll talk about that a year from now when our resort covers this whole crummy beach."

The man laughed. He waved. He swung the boat around and throttled toward the yacht. So far, the little motor was running fine. Over his shoulder he called out a threat. Something about "Don't call the police or I'll . . ."

Two miles offshore, the helicopter swooped lower. The pilot switched on a spotlight that only Luke noticed.

Red Beard kept going. Throttle open, the dinghy pushed a silver wake toward the yacht.

Tamarin approached the boy from behind, carrying his T-shirt and boots. He was wet, the lightning scar shiny on his shoulder.

"Better put these on or you'll catch cold." Tamarin

sounded a little shy. "I was worried about you and Maribel. The moon's too bright to be in the water this late. See any sharks?"

"Just one," Luke said. He ducked into his shirt, then stepped back. In Tamarin's other hand was the machete.

"How'd you get that?"

"Took it when that fella was in so much pain he needed our help," the local girl said. "Sabina found your first-aid kit. Somehow she convinced him that necklace of hers is magic. Silly, huh?"

Luke wasn't so sure after what happened next.

A few yards from the beach, the outboard motor finally ran out of gas. The dinghy began to drift back toward the sandbar.

Red Beard cussed the little motor and yanked on the starter cord.

"I warned you!" Sabina shouted. The girl was so mad she pulled away from Maribel and waded into the water. "Throw me my necklace, or Lucinda won't make the helicopter go away."

"Helicopter?" Red Beard replied. He was too focused on the engine to notice anything else. "Who the heck's Lucinda? You're nuts, you know that?"

He yanked the starter cord a couple more times. Nothing. When the current spun the dinghy toward shore, he stood as if to check the fuel tank.

Bad idea. Red Beard was a big man in a small rubber boat. For the first time, he noticed the chopper's searchlight speeding toward them. He panicked and lost his balance. The boat skidded from beneath his feet and he tumbled into the water.

Sabina splashed through the shallows after him.

Luke was moving, too. The tiger shark had heard the noise. In the shadow of the cliff, the gray fin pivoted and arrowed toward the beach.

"Grab your sister," he yelled to Maribel. "I'll try to find that old anchor."

Red Beard surfaced. The thumping *whomp-a-whomp* of the helicopter roared past overhead. The next thing the man saw was the tiger shark's fin. Like the blade of a knife, the fin carved a line through the moonlight toward his legs.

Sabina saw it, too. She backed away, slowly at first. "Get in the boat!" she ordered the man. "Do what I say!"

Red Beard lunged and got one arm over the side of the dinghy. Then he froze. He couldn't take his eyes off the giant fin cruising toward him. It was as if the man was hypnotized.

"Get in the boat!" the girl screamed again. "Hurry up!"

Behind her, Luke had found the old anchor. He coiled the blue nylon rope as Sabina shouted a new list of orders to the man. "Too late, don't move. Stop splashing! Okay, close your eyes. My spell will protect you if you do what I say!"

For an instant, Red Beard glanced at the girl. He looked helpless.

Promise? he seemed to ask. Then he obeyed. Jaw clenched, he closed his eyes when the tiger shark was only a few yards away.

The man didn't see the fin disappear beneath the water. And he didn't see Luke hurl the anchor. But he heard the splash near his head. Startled, Red Beard wrestled himself onto the rubber boat and lay back, exhausted.

The helicopter turned. From the lagoon, its searchlight found the dinghy. Sabina's voice pierced the thumping sound of the chopper's engines.

"Now do you believe me?" she yelled to the man. "My necklace, I want it. You better keep your promise, or I won't ever save you again!"

Because of the spotlight, it was like Red Beard was

onstage in some big theater. With a dazed expression, he got to his knees. In his hand was the string of cowrie shells.

"Throw them!" Sabina shouted.

The man did. Maribel retrieved the beads, then hustled her sister out of the water.

Red Beard faced the helicopter. He looked scared and desperate. He began to wave his arms to get attention. Even when the chopper hovered overhead, he continued to signal his location to the pilot.

Later, Luke, Tamarin, and the Estéban sisters were still confused about the man's behavior. Had he waved his arms in surrender? Or was he begging the government agents to rescue him from Sabina?

One thing they agreed on, though: Red Beard had been crying like a child.

THIRTY-NINE
SAYING GOODBYE
(Sabina and Luke)

Every night for a week, Sabina turned her bedcovers into a tent and tried to communicate with the ghost of Lucinda Bonny Rowland.

The brass picture frame, though, lacked warmth. There were no flutelike replies from the wind.

Lucinda's last words still echoed in the girl's head.

Keep my secret safe. You'll know what to do when you get there.

What secret? Get where?

Sabina still didn't understand.

Winifred Olivia Chase had told her, "You'll figure it out, kiddo. If you don't, we'll figure it out together after I meet with my attorney in Nassau."

That was three days ago.

Winifred had been working hard to save the Dilly Tree Inn. The casino company's loan had to be repaid in full soon. A single Spanish doubloon, as they all knew, wasn't worth nearly enough.

The next step was to prove that Tamarin's family owned all the land that had been granted to them by the king of England many years ago.

An important piece of evidence was Lucinda's gold wedding ring.

No one believed that a ghost had given Sabina the ring. Even the famous writer was convinced that the girl had found it while sleepwalking.

"Sometimes we get so involved in our dreams," Winifred had said, "it's hard to believe they're not real. What is real, my dear, is your unusual sensitivity. You have the greatest gift I've ever seen for finding small, lost treasures."

Winifred had snapped several photos of the ring, saying, "I'll be back on Thursday. By then I should know what the design on the ring means. Later, we'll visit Lucinda's grave. But don't get your hopes up. It's fun to pretend, but . . . well, let's be honest, kiddo. We both know that ghosts don't really exist."

On Thursday, Luke was up at dawn. Maribel and Sabina were so darn slow in the morning; it really was as irritating as having two sisters. So he was alone, snorkeling in the lagoon, long before breakfast.

In the week following Red Beard's capture, the boy had spent as much time by himself as possible. There was a reason. Soon they would have to return to Florida. He hated saying goodbye to people even more than he disliked meeting people.

The thought of saying goodbye made Luke uncomfortable. He could picture the hugs and handshakes that he would have to pretend to enjoy.

No thanks. Why did people get so emotional? In his mind, a simple wave was enough. It was better to just wander away and disappear.

Sneaking off alone hadn't been easy recently. The kids had been questioned by a nice detective. They had been interviewed by a reporter from a Bahamas radio station. To the people on Katt Island, he and the sisters were heroes.

Tamarin, too.

Instead of being arrested for poaching turtles, she and

some other local kids were credited with helping the police—thanks to Doc and the old preacher.

So, on this breezy August morning, Luke was glad to escape with his mask and fins. The tide floated him into the lagoon. The *click—boom . . . boom-boom* of lionfish warned there was a coral head nearby. Candy-colored clownfish browsed among tree roots. A school of snapper parted like a curtain.

Luke felt like an astronaut gliding among stars.

He had learned to recognize several types of sea turtles. Hawksbills had beautiful shells of jade and caramel. Green turtles weren't green; their shells were reddish brown, shaped like shields. Several glided past him, but the boy had learned not to follow.

Four days ago, he had led the famous writer to the Boiling Blue Hole. Next they had visited Whale Mouth Cave, where, finally, he had recovered his missing swim fin.

Winifred didn't understand how the lagoon was connected to the cave. Luke knew a way to demonstrate. At the Dilly Tree, he'd used the slab of limestone where, every night, a smudge fire was lit to keep bugs away. He stuck a hose in a crevice, waited a minute or so, and water streamed out of a dozen other holes.

"Brilliant," the old lady had said. "Tourists will love this place. When my magazine article is published, Katt Island and the Dilly Tree will be famous. And the book I'm writing will make them known around the world."

Luke had wanted to respond, *I hope we're gone by then*, but didn't. Why invite trouble?

After lunch on that Thursday, he felt the same when he saw Sabina. The girl was in a dreamy, stubborn mood. He could tell. Her face had a spooky violet glow. She was lugging her bag and a shovel down the beach toward the banana hole.

"Where're you going?" he asked. Immediately, the boy regretted the question.

"What's it matter?" Sabina responded. "You wouldn't believe me anyway. No one does. Everyone thinks I'm totally crazy—a little kid who walks in her sleep."

Luke knew he had to answer carefully. "Uh . . . I wouldn't say you're totally crazy. Just sometimes. Aren't you supposed to wait for Winifred? She and Doc will be back from Nassau soon with news from her attorney."

For some reason that made the girl mad. She scowled at him. "I'm not a little kid, you pig farmer. I'm not crazy, either. You'll see."

She threw her braids back and continued on toward the path to the ridge.

"What should I tell her?" Luke hollered.

"I'm tired of waiting," Sabina replied. "Winnie will know where to find me."

"The old mansion?" the boy guessed. "Hang on, I'll get my boots. You can't go wandering around up there all alone."

He was confused by Sabina's answer, which was "I won't be alone!"

Luke ran to his cabin, then followed the girl anyway.

FORTY
SAYING GOODBYE
(Maribel and Tamarin)

Maribel dreaded leaving Katt Island. Since that scary night on the beach with Red Beard and sharks, Tamarin had become the closest friend she'd ever had.

They could talk about anything. And they did. During their free time, they couldn't wait to slip out, just the two of them.

Both girls had grown up worried about their mothers and money problems. They each excelled at school, but both of them fretted that they weren't as smart as some believed. Pretending to be perfect, the girls agreed, got tiresome. It was an act—sometimes. But people they cared about depended on their solid behavior. Alone, though, just the two of them, they could say any silly, dumb thing that popped into their minds, and it was okay.

For Maribel, it was a new experience. The same with Tamarin. They'd had other friends, sure. But they had shared a terrifying night together. It was rare to find a person who had the same hopes and fears, and was willing to admit it.

The girls had laughed a lot during the last week. They'd gotten teary-eyed together. They had also revealed some of their most private secrets.

Friendship is mysterious. They were BFFs—a bond that couldn't be faked. It had to do with trust. No promises were required.

More than anything else, Maribel dreaded saying goodbye to Tamarin.

On that Thursday afternoon, the girls shared a hammock while waiting for Winifred Olivia Chase to change clothes. Doc's plane had landed an hour ago.

"Bet she has bad news about the Dilly Tree," Tamarin confided. "Why else would she speak privately to Mama first? Didn't say anything but 'hello' to us. Then asked about Sabina."

Maribel pointed out that Winifred had also asked about Preacher Josiah Bodden.

This gave the girls something to whisper about. Except for the trip to Nassau, Winifred had spent most of her time with Josiah. They did everything together—explored the island by boat, or walked the beach at night.

"Think folks as old as them can fall in love?" Tamarin asked. She flashed a mischievous smile.

Maribel smiled, too. It was a chance to discuss a difficult subject—money. In Cuba, she'd been embarrassed when tourists tossed coins to her and other poor kids, saying, "Buy some new clothes." Not that she and Sabina hadn't accepted the coins. They had. Sometimes. Not always.

It was rude to embarrass a friend, so Maribel had to be mindful. "If those two are in love, it explains why Winifred offered to invest money in the Dilly Tree. The loan could be paid off. I still don't understand why your mother said no."

"That's money *we* owe," Tamarin said. "No one else. The only reason Mama accepted the gold doubloon was because—well, you know the answer to that."

Sabina had found the coin in the banana hole. Doc and Hannah had argued that anything found on the ridge, by rights, belonged to Tamarin's family. It had taken a lot of convincing. Mrs. Rowland would not accept charity.

Which was why Maribel replied gently, "If Winifred wants to retire here, you'd be doing her a favor. I'd hate to come back and find them building some huge casino."

Tamarin's opinion of Katt Island had not changed. "There's nothing else for tourists to do here. Doesn't matter who owns the beach or the lagoon. If Mama and me don't find a way to pay off that loan, it really doesn't much matter if they—"

The girls were interrupted by the bang of a screen door.

Winifred Chase exited her cabin. She had changed from business attire into slacks and boots, and carried a hiking stick. Her necklace was a string of faded cowrie shells once owned by a girl named Lucinda Bonny Rowland.

"Where's Sabina?" the old lady asked. "We had a date to do some exploring this afternoon."

"Not sure, Ms. Winifred," Tamarin said. Then she couldn't help but ask, "What were you and my mother talking about so long? You got bad news in Nassau, I suppose."

Winifred shrugged in a sly way. But her triumphant smile said just the opposite was true.

Maribel spoke up. "I saw my sister on the beach more than an hour ago. Luke thought she was probably going to the mansion. He followed her, or I would've gone, too."

"The old cemetery, you mean," the famous writer said softly.

"Cemetery?" Maribel was concerned. "I hope not. She was carrying a shovel. You don't think my sister would—"

"Dig up a grave? No, of course not, dear. Josiah will be here in a minute. Why don't you girls put on some heavier shoes? Then we'll all go look for her."

The writer thought for a moment and looked fondly at Tamarin. "Your mother and I had a very nice talk. She's a wonderful woman, but I wish she weren't so stubborn."

Tamarin wondered if this was an insult.

"It's just like you told me," Winifred continued. "The king of England granted your family all of the lagoon, and miles of the most beautiful beach in the world. That's why I went to Nassau. My lawyer is sure he can prove it."

Tamarin's confusion vanished. "For real?"

The woman's tone became serious. "One thousand acres of land, my dear. But you need to convince your mother she needs an investor. Someone like me. And we need to come to an agreement very soon."

"I think you'd be a wonderful partner, ma'am," the local girl replied. "But Mama doesn't accept charity—or loans from friends. That's just the way she is."

Winifred understood, but warned, "Well, somehow you have to pay off the casino company's loan. If you don't, they'll take all the land, too. And there's nothing my lawyer can do to stop them." The woman paused, then added, "Besides, tell your mama my investment isn't charity. This place is special, and I want to be a part of that."

FORTY-ONE
DIGGING LUCINDA'S GRAVE

Luke followed Sabina from a distance. Going up the path to the banana hole, he was careful not to make noise. The same when she ducked through thorns into the opening where the old mansion lay in ruins.

He wasn't being sneaky. It was because of Sabina's behavior. He didn't want to embarrass the girl.

Every few hundred yards, she would stop and call, "Lucinda, I'm here! I know what you want me to do. But why?" Over and over, she stopped and spoke to the silence of a bright blue sky. The wording varied, but the question was always the same.

"Why?"

Luke didn't want to believe it, but he thought, *Maybe she is a tad crazy.*

Sabina hiked through weeds past the mansion to the small white gravestone. In the shade of a giant mango tree, she dropped the shovel and knelt. From her beach bag, she produced the old portrait in its brass frame. Next she opened the little black box she had found.

The girl mumbled a few words to the portrait, then removed a gold ring from her finger. Tenderly, as if tucking in a child, she placed the old portrait in the box. Atop the picture she put the ring, and then closed the lid.

For cripes' sake, Luke thought. *It's true. She's nuttier than three loons.*

The girl's attention shifted from the box to the gravestone. The marker stood alone, not much taller than the weeds.

Sabina stared and stared. It was as if she was sleepwalking again. Then, suddenly, she jumped to her feet and cried, "Lucinda . . . you're real, I know you're real!"

Her excitement had to do with something written on the marker.

Luke wanted to get a closer look. He left his thorny hiding place and slipped over the remains of a stone fence. Did it all without a sound—until he tripped over a branch and nearly fell.

Sabina whirled around. After a few seconds, the hopeful look on her face faded. Luke pretended to be invisible until she yelled, "I see you, farm boy. Get over here and help me."

Sheepishly, he got to his feet. "Help you do what?" he asked.

Sabina stood impatiently by the small white marker. She thrust the shovel into his hands and pointed. "Start digging," she said.

Dig up a grave?

Luke stepped back. In a way, he sort of liked the idea. Aside from a coffin and a skeleton, what else might they find? On the other hand, it sounded like a bad idea.

"I'm pretty sure grave robbing is illegal," he said. "What if we get caught? Maribel and the old lady might show up here any minute. I told her where you were going."

Sabina motioned to the small gravestone. A new inscription and a date had been carved into the weathered old stone. The girl tapped her toe, waiting. "Can't you read?"

The boy looked at the stone blankly. Finally, Sabina gave up. "You still don't understand, do you?"

Nope. And Luke didn't like it when she added, "It's a

good thing pigs and dogs think you're smart. We're not robbing Lucinda's grave, you coconut head. We need to dig a hole and bury this."

The small black box, Sabina meant.

"You sure there's not a coffin down there?" Luke asked.

"Maybe. Could be," was the reply. "But that's not what I'm looking for. There might be something else."

Sabina was thinking about the ghost of the beautiful teenager. Her husband, Alistar Katt, had taken something valuable from the murderous thieves as a wedding present for Lucinda.

Luke hefted the shovel. It was a rounded spade. A little rusty, but sharp enough. He thrust it into the ground. He jumped on the foot tang to bury the blade deeper.

Several times he did this before he heard the blade thunk against something hard. Metal, it sounded like.

"What is it?" Sabina got down and began clawing dirt away with her hands. "Mother of stars!" she exclaimed when she saw what they had found.

Luke was excited, too, but mostly relieved.

"I was afraid I'd dug up that dead girl's skeleton," he said. "Let's bury your box and get the heck out of here."

FORTY-TWO
FOREVER YOUNG

Winifred Olivia Chase was eighty years old. Preacher Bodden was probably older. Both were in good shape for their age.

Even so, Maribel and Tamarin allowed them several rest stops during the hike up the ridge to what was once a mansion.

On the way, Winifred talked about her trip to the big city of Nassau. She and her attorney had met with government officials. Documents found in the church, and the Rowland family Bible, had been presented as evidence.

"Photos of the wedding ring Sabina found," Winifred said to the girls, "are what finally convinced them."

It was complicated. The writer did her best to explain.

Three hundred years ago, the king of England had used a signet ring on documents to confirm ownership of land in the Bahamas. The ring given to Lucinda Bonny Rowland was etched with a similar symbol: an angel wearing a crown.

"Captain Arthur Katt, the old pirate, used that same symbol as his family crest," Winifred said. "The wedding ring given to Lucinda by his great-grandson, Alistar Katt, confirms they were married. That makes the bond legal. It proves that she should have inherited her husband's property after he was murdered."

The woman let that sink in. She touched her old necklace of cowrie shells. "But the Katt family refused to accept Lucinda. I think I know why. I'm still doing research, but it has to do with Lucinda's name."

Maribel had been following along closely. "Why? Lucinda is a beautiful name."

"Lucinda *Bonny* Rowland," Winifred said again with emphasis.

They continued toward the cemetery at a slow pace. On the way, Maribel and Tamarin listened to Winifred tell a pirate story. But it wasn't a story, because it was all true.

Three hundred years ago, Captain Anne Bonny was a famous pirate. She had commanded her own ship, and was feared by all. She and another pirate—a man called Blackbeard—were arrested.

"They hanged Blackbeard," Winifred explained. "But Captain Anne Bonny was pregnant. Even in those days, they didn't hang pregnant women, so they let her go, and she disappeared. I believe her child was born here on Katt Island."

Tamarin understood immediately. "Oh my gosh . . . I'm related to Lucinda Bonny," she murmured. "I get it. Rich folks didn't want their son to marry the poor daughter of a pirate—even though their family got rich by robbing ships and stealing land."

"Lucinda was probably Anne Bonny's great-granddaughter," Winifred said. "You can be proud to be part of her family. Captain Bonny was headstrong and independent. A fierce warrior."

Tamarin was still in a funk about the loan her mother couldn't repay. "Then one of her kids or grandbabies must'a married into the Rowland family. And we're even poorer. Nothing but bad luck in the Rowland clan. That's the way it's always been."

The old man, Preacher Bodden, hadn't said much, but he had to smile. "Young lady," he said, his voice a cheerful grumble, "we live in one of the most beautiful places on this good Earth. Don't you give up. There are mysteries aplenty on this island."

He exchanged a fond wink with Winifred.

By then they were at the mansion's old cemetery. Sabina and Luke were visible in the distance. They were on their knees next to a small white marker.

"What in the world are those coconut-head kids doing?" Tamarin wondered.

They stopped for a moment and watched in disbelief. Sabina, in a rush, was dropping what might have been rocks into her beach bag. Luke was using a shovel to smooth a mound of freshly turned soil.

Maribel was horrified. "This is terrible. They couldn't have!"

"Yes, they did," Tamarin said. "Dug up that dead woman's grave. And she's my poor blessed relative. Let's go see."

Running, they left the old couple behind.

When Sabina saw the girls coming, she jumped to her feet. Her beach bag was so heavy, she couldn't drag it out of sight. "Help me lift this thing," she whispered to Luke. "I don't want them to see what we found. Not yet."

The boy was tired of being bossed around. "Why? They're bound to know sooner or later." He was thinking, *Crazy as three loons. Yep.*

Sabina grunted and strained, but managed to move the bag only a few inches. "Hurry up," she ordered. "They'll be here in a few seconds. I want Winnie to see Lucinda's gravestone first. She'll notice what you didn't notice. And she'll never accuse me of sleepwalking again."

Luke didn't bother with another glance at the white marker. Instead he dropped the shovel and grabbed the bag by both straps. Using his legs, he hefted it off the ground.

"Holy moly," he muttered. "This thing isn't that heavy. A bale of hay weighs a lot more. But I don't think this bag is strong enough to—"

As he spoke, the cloth handles snapped. The contents of the bag spilled out onto the fresh grave of a young woman who was finally at peace.

Maribel got there first. Her anger vanished when she saw what had happened.

Tamarin was stunned, too. Glittering at Luke's feet were dozens of gold coins.

"A hundred Spanish doubloons—minus one," Sabina announced. "They were a wedding gift to Lucinda on the night her husband was murdered. She wants Tamarin to have them because she's all the family that beautiful dead girl has ever had."

"Me?" Tamarin felt like she was dreaming. "Who you talking about?"

Winifred and Preacher Bodden arrived.

"Lucinda Bonny Rowland," the famous writer answered in a bold voice. She was reading what was engraved on the small white marker. "'Even in Death, Forever Young.'"

Maribel noticed the old couple joining hands.

Winifred squinted and moved closer to the small stone. She stared. Her eyes widened because the grave marker was different from before. The woman leaned and whispered something to the preacher that sounded like *Did you do this?*

Josiah Bodden, with a slight smile, only shrugged. "Already told you, Winnie, darlin'. This here is one mysterious island."

Winifred took another look at the words etched long ago into stone. She faced Sabina. "This is impossible, my dear! Someone with a chisel has added two new lines. But . . . the engraving doesn't look new."

Sabina folded her arms as if victorious after battle. "Now do you believe me?" the girl demanded. "This whole time, I've only been wrong about one thing—thirteen is *not* an unlucky number."

The gravestone, faded by wind and a hundred years of longing, read:

Lucinda Bonny Rowland
Beloved Wife of Captain Alistar Katt
Born: June 9, 1891
Died: Friday, August 13, 1910

Acknowledgments

Before thanking those who contributed their expertise, time, and good humor during the writing of *Stingers*, I want to make clear that all errors, exaggerations, or misstatements of fact are entirely the fault of the author. This applies to those good people who shared their expertise about the Bahamas, particularly Cat Island, which in this book I have fictionalized as Katt Island. The story line required the change because I had to stray too far afield from the island's actual history, and certain locations (such as Whale Mouth Cave and the Boiling Blue Hole) are real places, so they were intentionally disguised to protect the confidences shared by friends.

For this book, a key source of fact and lore was Capt.

Mark Keasler, an eco-fishing guide who has lived on Cat Island for more than thirty years. We met in 1995 and were the first to dive a spot known locally as "The Horse Eating Hole" because, we were told, it was where dead livestock were dragged and eaten overnight by something—a dragon, old-timers claimed. "A crocodile, more likely," Mark suggested. He not only provided a rubber raft but joined me in the lunacy of hacking our way to a pond that locals avoided day and night—no footpaths, no litter, no human spore of any kind.

Spooky? You bet.

Years ago, "Uncle Mark," as he is known on the island, founded the Barracuda Swim Club, a free program devoted to teaching children ecology, local history, and the importance of learning to swim. If he reminds you of Uncle Josiah in this novel, so be it. Child by child, things are changing on Cat Island. If you'd like to fish or explore with Capt. Mark in the Bahamas, contact him at bwanacat@yahoo.com.

Tony Ambrister, his family, and Wayne and Todd Timmerman of Fernandez Bay were also a great help. Unlike fictional Katt Island, the bay, with its crystalline water and white beaches, is among the safest places in the world and my favorite spot for open-water swimming and snorkeling.

I am also in debt to friends I met at Ms. Karen's Starlite Restaurant, the Hidden Treasures Restaurant, and to author Anishka Deveaux-King and family. They were generous with their time and stories of Bahamian lore.

I also owe thanks to my Cat Island Masonic brothers, Dominique Gibson of Nassau and Jovann O'Neil Burrows of Mount Alvernia Lodge, a fourth-generation Cat islander. They donated a lot of time, information, and fun to the writing of this book. It is a kindness I hope to repay.

—Randy Wayne White
Sanibel Island, Florida